PRINCE OF FLIGHT
(KING OF PREY)

A Bird Shifter Novel

MANDY M. ROTH

King of Prey Series

King of Prey
A View to a Kill
Master of the Hunt
Rise of the King
Prince of Pleasure
Prince of Flight

Blurb

This bad-boy biker beast has met a beauty
who isn't scared off by what she sees.

Chapter One

"SITTING AT THE BIG BOY TABLE NOW? YOU normally like that back corner one that only seats two. Or would seat two if you let anyone get near you."

Keonae glanced up from his seat in the back poolroom of the small roadside bar he enjoyed frequenting of late. He'd been a full-time resident in the human realm for far longer than the bar had been in existence, and the bar, as obvious from its state of decay, had seen many years.

"Cat got your tongue?"

He did all he could to remain calm as the beauty before him spoke. The mere sound of her voice held his full attention.

He could listen to her talk all day and all night. Hell, she could babble about anything and he'd hang on her every word.

Be ice.

That was what humans often said to one another, wasn't it? Or was it be wet? Be sub-zero? Be Artic? Perhaps be cool? He couldn't remember, nor could he keep track of all their slang.

Stupid humans with their ridiculous sayings.

He should know the human sayings well, like he knew the handle of his sword, but he did not take the time to commit them to memory. They seemed to change so very often. Humans had taken a nearly adequate language and butchered it long ago, and he had been around long enough to see it devolve at a rapid pace.

They had a saying or slang for nearly everything, and all of it took from the beauty of the words. From their meaning. His native tongue was nothing they would ever understand, even though Latin had been born from it long ago, as had several other languages the humans used. That was in the days when they foolishly thought his kind to be angels, gods— demons even.

Humans were not the smartest of races, that was for certain. He didn't mind them so much. They had grown on him over the centuries. Especially the human close to him now.

Yes. Be ice. Do not show her how she makes you feel. Do not reveal that she reminds you of the sweet summers near the edges of the springs of the Tocalie Mountains. That her scent is like that of the mavabian flowers that dotted the outer regions.

He wanted to wax poetic with her, show her he was more than he appeared, but he didn't dare. Romancing her wasn't an option.

Be ice. Be so cold your cock shrivels.

Somehow thinking it did little to settle him or his raging hard-on. Not with her being so close. Lark—such a beautiful name for such a beautiful woman—had a way of drawing his thoughts like no other. Of making him feel like a mere fledgling, rather than a man of many centuries. He was a man of high birth, of position and of power, should he ever decide to return to his place among his people in Accipitridae.

Sweat broke out on his palms. He'd never had sweaty palms prior to meeting her. The hold she had over him was spellworthy. Lark had been calling to him on a baser level from the moment he'd laid eyes on her nearly a month prior. He licked his lower lip. He wanted to sample her lips, but he didn't dare. Deep down he knew one taste would never be enough, and he wasn't the type of man who could have something long term.

At least not with a human woman.

"I await friends on this evening," he said, before clearing his throat, reminding himself his speech patterns were unusual when not tempered. "I'm waiting for *the guys*."

"Guys' night, Keon?" she asked, seeming to prefer to shorten his name down from Keonae. He would not have tolerated such a thing from any other than her. She smiled and it was both innocent and sexy all wrapped up in one. His dick responded in kind, lengthening, wanting to be in her. His breathing increased as desire lanced through him.

"Sweet," she added.

He mentally counted to twenty before speaking, worried his next words would be something along the lines of a sexual proposition, or even a flat-out decree that she bed him. While he wasn't opposed to making them, he didn't want to with her— not this woman. She was special. His old ways weren't ones he wanted to go back to in regards to Lark. "Yes. One of my brothers is coming as well."

"Really?" she asked, easing closer, excitement aglow on her face. He lived for these types of moments. Times when she'd smile for him. "I'll finally get to meet some of your friends and family? I was starting to think you might be making them up."

He pressed a partial smile to his face. He and Lark had done as he'd never done with a human before—they'd conversed on a deeper level more than once. He'd even shared some details of his friends and family—nothing about being a bird shifter from another realm, though.

"They'll be here soon," he said, his voice low. He wet his lips and glanced up at her, every ounce of him wanting to make contact with her.

She beamed. "Good. You need more people around you. You're always alone."

She was a fine one to talk. He'd noticed Lark didn't ever seem to have anyone close to her—unless he counted himself. They'd taken to going out to breakfast together when her shifts ended in the wee hours of the morning. They talked about everything and seemingly nothing at all. And they never talked about certain things. Things she wouldn't understand as a human.

But the one thing Keonae took note of was that she avoided discussing friends or family. She was as alone as he was. Maybe more.

"I'd like you to meet the guys when they get here." The statement was huge for more than one reason. He never let anyone meet others of his kind and he had certainly never introduced a human woman to them. At least, not since he'd taken the back-stabbing wench he'd once thought he loved before his brothers.

Lark nodded, her long, blonde hair spilling in all directions. "Of course."

Keonae sipped his beer as she headed back through the doorway to the main area of the bar, leaving him to sit alone, the way he preferred it. Several minutes passed before the men he'd been waiting on arrived. He lifted his beer as fellow bird shifters took seats around him at the circular table.

The bar was a hole in the wall, but Keonae preferred those to others. Most humans never asked him questions, and nearly all just let him be. To them, he was the brooding man who played darts or pool, who drank alone and who had the scar on his face. Very few were brave enough to ask how he got it. Those who did chance his wrath regretted their decision instantly. He wasn't one for sharing. That feel-good bullshit he saw on television, where everyone wanted to sit around in a circle and jerk each other off emotionally, wasn't for him. He wasn't one of those soft men—he was a warrior, and warriors weren't pussies.

The bar served another purpose, beyond just giving him a place to get drunk. If a bar fight erupted, as was often the case with the place, he was able to get some fighting in. It kept his skills honed. Coupled with his workouts, he stayed fit and active, always ready should the need to fight a real battle arise. Once, in his past, he'd been ill-prepared and arrogant, a young fool full of ideas of love and romance.

At the very thought of romance, he felt a tugging in his chest, his gaze moving to the doorway Lark had gone through. He would be lying to himself if he didn't admit that one of the main reasons he selected this particular hole in the wall was its staff. Lark, in particular.

Do not take your thoughts there, he scolded himself. *She, like all women, will only bring you pain and misery.*

He touched the side of his face that

bore the aftermath of his foolishness. He had a forever reminder to never go back to being that man. To never soften to anyone, especially not a woman who would only betray him in the end.

Keonae had very few regrets over leaving the bird realm. Missing the bouts of conditioning with his brothers and the guards of Accipitridae was one of them. They'd spend hours working out on the castle grounds, sparring and training. It wasn't easy to find anyone in the human realm willing or able to take up a sword and train with him. Most would just think he was a madman if he even inquired on it.

He looked down at his hand. It too held myriad scars, telling something of his tale. Flexing his fingers, he thought about what it was like to hold his sword, the feel of it in his hand, the weight of it.

"Hand hurt?" asked Rossi, his youngest brother. Rossi took a seat near Keonae. "Is it acting up again?"

Keonae grabbed his beer and chugged it before belching and setting it on the table, extending the fingers on his hand and giving a pointed look that said all was fine, stop asking.

Rossi snorted. "My apologies, my lord. I forgot. Everything is perfect in your world. Got it, *dickhead*."

"For someone living back in Accipitridae, you sound very human," said Keonae with wink. "You almost sound local."

"Ah, well, you're calling this place home, so take a bite out of me," returned Rossi as he grabbed one of the unopened beers and helped himself to it.

"I believe the correct phrase is 'bite me'," said Keonae with a half-laugh. "Correct me if I'm wrong, but didn't you used to spend an awful lot of time in this realm?"

Rossi used to troll the clubs for women. He'd been quite the ladies' man until he'd met his mate, and she'd changed him on the spot. The man now only had eyes for her. As it should be with a true mated pair. At least, that was what had been beaten into his head from birth. His father had been a firm believer in prophecy, big into chosen ones and mates. While a few of his brothers and friends had found their special some-one, it didn't mean anything to Keonae.

He was the leper of his family. The brother who was scarred and no longer pleasing to the eye, as they all had once been. In a society where physical beauty was so prized, their father had always put such stock in how handsome his boys were. How the females adored them and men feared them. As if fate wasn't cruel enough to leave most of his body so hideously scarred in some fashion from the attack, he had been born to the first set of multiples his mother had. He was a triplet. Two identical reminders of what he would no longer ever be, of what he once was, walked the bird realm.

And one was king.

No.

While Kabril and Aeson had been blessed with mates, the fates would not give him one. The gods could not be so cruel as to hand him a woman meant for him, only to have her shriek in horror and run from him, the monster.

He exhaled deeply, wanting the meeting to be over. He had no interest in the politics of home, yet his brothers continued to drag him into it, as if including him would make him want to return home and assume his place in the royal family.

It would not.

"What matters are we to discuss today?" he asked, bored already and the meeting had yet to start.

Rossi glanced around the back room of the bar. "I vote we talk about your choice for a meeting place. As much as I enjoy coming to the human realm, this place is a dump, even for me. You should just come home. I really don't understand what the big deal is. It has been how many decades since everything happened? Surely, you're over it."

I'll never go back and I'll never get over it.

The very thought of returning to the bird realm made him look in the direction of the doorway. In the direction he knew *her* to be in.

Odd.

He hoped he wasn't growing attached to her in a way that would make him unwilling to uproot and find a new place to call home within the human realm. He long ago ceased to age, which made it necessary, after a period, to find a new location to live within the human world. They aged. They died. They'd notice if he didn't.

"You know why he does not return, Rossi," Sachin said from his seat next to Keonae. "Your brother does his best to avoid setting foot upon home soil. It holds too many memories."

Thoughts of his dead betrothed hit him hard. She used to beg to be brought to the human realm, to be near her mother's people, but Keonae had always refused her. He'd thought her whims foolish and her desires to escape the bird realm nothing more than something that would pass. It had not. And he'd had no idea the lengths she'd end up going to in order to achieve her desires.

"Of a dead traitor? Of a woman who was a mix of our kind, a blend of human and shifter yet worthy of neither race? A half-breed who sought fame and wealth and who, in the end, nearly cost us you?" Rossi questioned.

Keonae knew the words were spoken, not out of truth, but rather fear. Rossi's mate, a human herself, was now expecting their first children. She was late in the term and had been sick for the majority of it. From what Keonae had been told by his other brothers, Rossi had taken to visiting the seers nearly daily for assurance his wife and their babes would be fine come delivery day. The weight of worry was heavy upon the man. Keonae knew what that felt like, so he made no motion to correct his brother's offense. Rossi was right, after all. Ultimately, his betrothed had been a traitor and a blend from a human and shifter mating. The first chance she had to align with the falcons, who had promised her riches and a one-way ticket to the human realm, she took, and betrayed Keonae when he was fighting for his own life, unable to assist. He had watched her die and he had laid there, assuming he too would perish.

Lazar, a relative newcomer to the advisory council meetings, sat up, his blond hair hanging over one eye. He appeared offended on Keonae's behalf. "Your over-simplification does insult to your brother's pain. It is memories of a woman who betrayed him to spy for my people, giving herself to them freely, and in the end betrayed by them and given over to vultures, who killed her slowly."

Keonae tried to remain hard and detached from the words spoken. It was difficult. The wounds long since healed as much as they ever would, burned anew, the remembered pain there, just below the surface. Worse yet were the emotions—the rage, the hate, the humiliation. Feelings he never wanted to have again.

"They were not your people," Sachin said matter-of-factly. The man always kept a level head about him. Well, unless his mate was involved and then it was anyone's guess how his temperament would be. "You have proven you are nothing like your brethren, Lazar. You are nothing like Latravis or those who support him in his reign of terror. Keonae realizes as much, or he would not permit you to attend these meetings."

"You are not your brother," said Keonae evenly. "And while I do not condone violence against women, she made her choices. She knew the people she was getting into bed with. She knew they were not to be trusted."

"Half-brother," corrected Lazar, the distinction clearly of importance to him. Keonae couldn't blame him. Latravis was touched in the head and said to be unraveling at rapid pace, though word at the last few meetings was that he had changed his wicked ways and was trying to start anew.

The idea made Keonae laugh.

The *Falco Peregrinus*, whom Lazar belonged to, and Keonae's family, the *Buteos Regalis*, or royal hawks, had been at war for centuries. Though the battles had become few and far between in the latter decades, a new war was brewing. Talk of troops moving on borders had consumed their meetings for the past year. Random raids and failed attempts at peace appeared to be the new normal.

Why would he want to go back to that?

Drinking in the human realm was much better.

"I know not how you can break bread with me," said Lazar to Keonae. "I must represent everything and everyone you hate."

"You remind me of the past in some ways, but you give me a spark of hope that the old ways will not always be so," said Keonae, drawing a look of surprise from Sachin.

It was true. He knew the truth of Lazar. He was rightful king of the Falconi. Soon, they'd make a move and help him regain the throne from his twisted half-brother. In the meantime, they were busy fighting off recent attacks on the edges of their kingdom from the vultures.

Keonae glanced around the table.

"Dare I ask what the vultures have been up to? It's bad enough they seem to rise from obscurity, but now it is as if they have a hand in nearly all that is going wrong back home."

Chapter Two

THE MEN PRESENT SHARED CONCERNED looks, probably fearing he might break upon hearing anything in the way of news on the vultures. Keonae lifted a hand. "Worry not. I have put the past behind me and will not shatter to pieces with talk of them. I asked because I wish to know and because I sense you've been leaving a lot out of our last meetings in regards to them."

Sachin cleared his throat. "We believe we can account for their large numbers."

Keonae waited, saying nothing more.

Sachin glanced to Lazar and then to Keonae, hesitant to speak further.

"Tell me."

"It is merely a theory for now," said Sachin.

Rossi spat to the side, cursing the bird gods before returning to ranting about the vultures. "Carcass feeders!"

Lazar lifted his beer to toast the statement. "Agree. They are bottom dwellers."

Most had assumed the vultures had permanently tucked themselves away to lick their wounds from the wars of two centuries ago. Some were even rumored to have fled to the human realm to escape being tried for war crimes. Keonae himself could attest to the vultures being comfortable with passing between realms—he'd been ambushed by them upon human soil and that was why he had not healed as he should have. On Accipitridae, he would have been left whole, perfect as he had once been, not marred. Not still with pain at random times. He should have had full mobility. He didn't.

It had been hoped the vultures' numbers had dwindled as had those in most of the bird kingdoms. Those hopes had been dashed in recent months as verification of the increase in vulture numbers came to a head. They were attacking all kingdoms within the bird realm and in numbers that took everyone by surprise. It was clear they had successfully overcome the low birth rates that had beleaguered the realm for so long.

They were poised to be a serious threat to Accipitridae once more. Keonae touched his scars gently and then let his hand fall away to avoid bringing attention to them. Vultures had left their mark on him, a permanent reminder of their cruelty.

"What theory do you have on their numbers being so high when all the rest of the realm struggles so with new births?" asked Keonae.

The men were quiet for far too long and Keonae knew the information they had was not good. It was Lazar who finally spoke. "They have found a way to artificially breed. They have perfected this over the last century through aid of human technologies in the fields of reproduction, DNA cloning, and something they refer to as genetic engineering. Kabril is meeting with a team of scientists from here, learning all he can of this."

"They played gods?" inquired Keonae, his breath nearly stolen at the idea of something as sick and vile as vultures managing to create an army from scratch. "They did this within the realm?"

Rossi shook his head. "Not all of it. No. From what we are learning most took place here in remote locations. We know very little beyond this."

Keonae found himself lost in worry and thoughts, his mind a mess and his body tense and tight. After a while, he noticed no one else dared to speak, giving him time to absorb the news.

"Are you well?" asked Sachin.

Keonae nodded. "Reflecting on matters best left in the past."

"Hard to keep it behind you when we come and set it before your table, yes?" asked his friend.

Keonae slid him a knowing look. "I need to be kept abreast of the situation back home, regardless of what that situation may be. How many more attacks have been reported?"

"A half-dozen. Rossi confirmed it was vultures because he had to engage with them. He managed to capture one who gave confirmation of what we had only recently learned. They bred an army."

He looked to his younger brother. "And?"

"I walked away alive, unlike some who were with me," Rossi said softly. "They died honorable deaths. They fought for their kingdom."

Lazar stiffened in his seat. "The eagles have sent reinforcements to help us with our borders."

"Are their own not at risk?" asked Keonae.

Sachin shook his head. "Not at this time. And their numbers are greater than our own. They have offered the falcons assistance as well, but only after assuring Kabril would not take offense."

Keonae snorted. "They do not want Kabril carrying a grudge. He is much like our father."

The men all agreed.

"The owls have reached out as well. Seems they are willing to assist. I believe they do not like knowing the vultures have gained knowledge over them," said Sachin.

Keonae laughed. "And pull themselves from their never-ending quest for knowledge? I am shocked. Will they throw books at the vultures? Beat them to death with scrolls?"

Rossi laughed and drank more beer. "They have already tried to convince the queen a more rigorous education should be in order for the newly birthed children within the realm."

"Oh, of that I have no doubt. Our tutors when we were young fledglings were all of the owl kingdom. Do you recall?"

Rossi groaned. "Yes. Do not remind me."

Keonae was surprised to hear the owls had joined against the vultures. They thought themselves scholars, too smart and above war to be bothered. But they knew the stories of old—of a time when the vultures ruled the realm—and it was not a good era for the shifters.

Not in the least.

Each kind tended to stick to themselves and handle their own conflicts. It took a serious matter for peace between the races, regardless of how fragile it was, to be reached. Although, Keonae doubted very much anything in the way of peaceful negotiations would happen with Lazar's people. Not with tensions as high as they were.

"Remember when Aeson was unhappy with his history lessons and decided to pull pranks on the tutor?" asked Rossi, talking of their brother.

"I do. Father scolded him and required he clean chamber pots for a solid week."

Sachin laughed. "Speaking of Aeson, was he not to meet us here tonight as well?"

Lazar nodded. "He told me he would meet us here. We assumed he would be here, in the bar."

Keonae grunted. "He's not. He's probably home bedding his mate. That seems to be his favorite pastime anymore. If that is what he calls fun, fine."

"I should be home with mine," Lazar added, grinning. "Trust me when I say she looks better than all of you put together."

The others razzed him about his wife, whom they all liked. Keonae didn't have an opinion of her as he'd not had the pleasure of actually meeting her. The others spoke highly of Lazar's woman. That was all that mattered to him.

"This talk makes me thankful I have no mate to speak of." Keonae finished the beer and opened another. "I have no one to answer to. I am free to live my life as I wish. Kick back and enjoy drink and no commitments." At the very thought of commitments his mind centered on Lark. He would answer to her if she would have him, but the problem was she never would. She was too good for him. Too beautiful, kind, and caring.

More than he deserved and more than he dared hope for. In addition, she was human, and humans and his kind only worked if they were true mates. The gods would not grant him one. Not with his past sins.

In some ways, he'd gotten what he deserved. He'd bloodied his sword too many times to count. He'd killed the enemy even when they begged for their lives, and when one requested a quick death, he denied them as much, making them suffer. There had been a time when he was one of the most feared of the hawks' warriors. Bloodthirsty and bent on winning as all warriors were, he'd been ruthless in his quest for victory in battle. But in the end, he'd been blinded by lust, then nearly blinded for real. The bird gods demanded payment due, and payment he had made.

"I still cannot fathom why we're meeting in this dive," said Rossi. "Aeson has raised his standards. He probably showed, took one look at this place, and then fled. Smart man."

"Hey, I like this bar. It is one of my favorites," he said, omitting the fact that it was only his favorite because of Lark.

"You have been living as a human for

far too long if this bar holds appeal," said Sachin. "Your standards have fallen greatly."

Had they not been friends all their lives, Keonae would have taken offense. As it stood, he knew Sachin's words were birthed out of concern and a healthy grain of truth. The bar *was* a hole in the ground.

Lifting his beer, Keonae inclined his head to make a toast. "To using women to serve one's needs so long as I'm not tethered to a mate, and to dives like this. May the shit hole-in-the-ground places always welcome a motley crew such as us."

Rossi's sound of disgust wasn't lost on Keonae. "Brother, tell me you're not planning to continue living here in this realm. More to the point, near this place. The human realm is a wonderful place to visit, but to lay roots? To call home? Also, I believe the human term for this is hole-in-the wall, not ground."

Sachin groaned. "Rossi has moaned since our departure. Mayhap the moons back home are afflicting him."

"Make fun of humans," said Lazar to

Rossi before he drank his beer. "I dare you. I will tell your wife. Lucy will unman you."

"Hey, none of that now," said Rossi with wide eyes. "Her moods have been sour enough with me of late. She needs no encouragement. I had no idea human females could be so violent. Pregnancy has made her scary. I show no fear in battle, yet I shake in her presence. I spent last night sleeping upon the floor outside our chamber doors as she deemed me in the dog house, whatever that means. Humans are very strange beings."

"My wife just happens to be human too. As does your queen," reminded Sachin. "If they hear you talking about their tempers, they'll team up with Lucy and they'll all geld you." Sachin leaned forward as if daring Rossi to say more. Wisely, Rossi shut up.

Keonae laughed, bringing a look of surprise from the males around him. "What? I find it humorous that you are all terrified of *little* human women."

"You really need to meet them face-to-face," said Sachin. "They'd scare the feathers off a vulture."

Keonae smiled wide and felt the pull on the right side of his face from muscles he didn't use often. He quickly schooled his expression, dreading drawing attention to his misshapen smile.

"Speaking of vultures," said Lazar, knocking lightly on the table. "You were correct, Keonae. We have held much back from you in the past months."

Keonae nodded, figuring as much.

Lazar continued. "They have been attacking on the edges of the kingdom, we believe in an attempt to test our forces and our protection lines. To date, they have not been successful in gaining access to the hawks' area, but I do not think that is their true mission."

Sachin let out a long breath. "Nor do I. They seek to distract us while testing our resolve."

"Bottom feeders," mouthed Rossi.

Lazar nodded. "Word reached us that they're planning a raid here in the human realm. And if our spies are correct, this raid is to occur not far from where you lay your head, Keonae. And we do not believe it will be far in the future."

"I would like to place guards with you until this blows over," said Sachin, tipping his head. "I know you will protest and tell me no, but think upon it. You are not the seasoned warrior you once were. You have lived the way of a human for far too long to stand alone against a threat such as them."

"Says you," added Keonae, knowing he hadn't just withdrawn from the fight and lost his edge. If anything, he worked harder, trained harder, and spent more time preparing for a battle that may never come. The blood thirst that had once been his driving force was no more. That had been beaten out of him and died the day his world changed forever. But upon reflection, he knew it would make him a better warrior. One who could stand against a foe and not allow the thrill of the kill be what guided his actions.

Rossi lifted his beer. "We first assumed they were making a move upon you, trying to draw us out, but then new information came to light—they seek a woman."

Keonae wasn't following. "What would they want with a human woman? They have never been known to show an interest in this realm before. When they ruled supreme, the portals were banned. What has changed?"

"That, we do not know," Sachin said, leaning back in his chair. "It is troublesome. They show the females of our realm no mercy when they capture one, so think of what horrors they could inflict upon a human woman. Consider allowing the guards to be placed near you. It would set all our minds at ease. Should the vultures make a move upon you, they will be able to assist."

Keonae flinched at the thought of the enemy getting their hands on a human woman. They were ruthless, and if they had human women in their sights, something was very wrong. Keonae had become protective of the humans to some degree, feeling as though he was part of them now, even though he doubted highly that any human would accept what he was. Should they realize he could sprout wings and fly, they would probably shoot him first and then examine his dead remains later. Humans were like that.

Except for one human female he found himself very drawn to. The idea of the vultures being anywhere near Lark set him on edge. The urge to stand and seek her out was strong, but just then, she came to him. His heart fluttered and he had to temper his breathing to avoid alerting his companions to just how much the woman meant to him.

Chapter Three

THE DOOR FROM THE MAIN AREA OF THE bar opened and Lark appeared, carrying a tray full of beers. Her long, blonde hair was pulled up haphazardly, falling in sexy, loose sections around her face. She stood tall for a human female, just under six feet with her heeled boots on. He liked that. Liked knowing there was a chance he could fuck her while standing. Not that he'd done more than converse with her to date. Still the fantasy remained, always lingering just below the surface, teasing him. Jeans fit her long legs and hugged her tight ass, only serving to turn him on more.

She'd only been working at the bar for

about four weeks, and in that time Keonae found himself frequenting the place more than previously. Nearly nightly to be exact. He craved her, wanting to simply occupy the same space as she. Lark had a softness that made him want to wrap her in his arms and protect her. And she enjoyed talking with him, though he knew not why. He was hardly a man of interest, yet she seemed to hang on his every word, as he did hers. She had a certain pull over him, one he didn't necessary like, but one he couldn't deny.

He was attracted to her in a way he'd not been attracted to a woman in nearly a century. He normally had no problem telling a woman if he wanted to fuck her. With Lark, however, he had issues even allowing her to see him in any sort of direct light, fearful she'd do as every woman did when seeing him in full light for the first time.

Flinch and recoil.

There had been a time, long ago, when women spoke of how handsome he was, how attractive. He was now hideous—a scarred mess of a man who had wanted nothing more than to hide away in the human realm and leave the past far behind him.

"Are you even listening?" asked Rossi.

Keonae tipped his head. No, he'd not bothered paying attention. His focus was still upon Lark as she came deeper into the back room, paying him little mind as she adjusted a tray of drinks. He'd wanted to show her off to the men, but now that they were here, he simply wanted them to go so he could spend time with her. He didn't want their judging gazes upon him.

He wanted to go to her, touch her, be touched by her, but he didn't dare move from his chair. Tonight he felt on edge, too close to doing something questionable. He could stand rejection from others, not that it lasted long, but he couldn't risk the look in Lark's eyes when she caught sight of him fully. She was different. He needed her to accept him for who and what he was, though it made no sense to him.

"I daresay your brother is ignoring you," interrupted Lazar with a snort as he found amusement in something. "He must feel you babble endlessly as well. We *all* share that opinion, Rossi."

Sachin laughed. "That we do."

Rossi followed Keonae's gaze and lifted a brow when he looked in Lark's direction. "I would take offense, but I think something else holds his interest."

"Or rather *someone*," stressed Lazar, noticing Lark as well.

Uncomfortable knowing the men had seen his keen interest in Lark, Keonae attempted to find his place within the conversation once more. "Vultures, yes. They're evil, vile pricks. We should string them all up. Blah, blah. What are we doing about them?"

The men shared a look and laughed.

"Oh yes," said Sachin. "Someone else holds his attention. Dear friend, we were taking a moment from talk of enemies to discuss the coming festivals. It would mean a great deal to Kabril to have all of us home for it. Though, I highly suspect your interests do not lie within festivals unless the celebration was to be held between a tall blonde's legs."

Keonae didn't comment because Lark picked then to approach their table. Her gaze found him and he averted his, trying to keep the scarred side of his face in the shadows of the dimly lit area at the end of the table.

"Keon," she said, holding her tray of beers. "I brought refills for you and your guys."

His hand went up to the top of his head, touching the black do-rag he wore that came down far, just missing covering his eyes. It hid a large portion of his scar. The rest of the scar was locked in the shadows as he kept his head bent, only showing the unmarred side of his face to her. It was hard to always try to hide his imperfections from her, but he did so anyway.

"*Keon?*" Rossi repeated in a mocking tone, and Keonae considering knocking his baby brother out of his chair.

"Enough, *Rossi*," Sachin scolded,

keeping his lips pressed in a thin line, appearing amused by it all even though he was trying not to.

The Keonae of old would have punched his youngest brother in the face by this point. The new man, brought about by the blonde he'd been coming to the bar in hopes of catching glimpses of, was a changed man. At least, he was trying to be.

"Lark," Keonae said, acknowledging her with the slightest of head inclines. "These are some of the motley crew I told you about. Sachin, Lazar, and my brother Rossi."

"Ah, one of the seven brothers," she said, grinning at Rossi. "I would have guessed that. The two of you look alike. Well, except for the eyes. And the fact you don't seem to give off the 'I will break you in two' vibe your brother here does."

Rossi gave him a questioning look, but said nothing.

"You've told her of your family?" Sachin asked, his underlying question clear. All eyes tracked to Keonae, as if the men in his company could not fathom that he would disclose anything to a woman, let alone personal information. Their gazes held concern. He knew why. They all held the same question on the tips of their tongues. What else had he confessed to her? That he was an immortal, able to shift into a hawk and that he wasn't from this realm?

No.

But he had told Lark of his brothers, as much as he could. He didn't think adding the fact they could shift into large birds, take flight, and were in a sense immortal would go over without a lot of questions and possibly a trip to the mental ward.

"Kabril is the oldest, right?" Lark asked, balancing the tray on her hip, her smile still spread across her face. "Then Aeson, with Keonae rounding out the triplets? Then two sets of twins and the end one, Rossi, right?" She moved up close to Keonae and, unable to restrain himself any longer after wanting to make contact with her for a month, he snaked an arm around her waist, his hand settling on her hip, nearly engulfing it. He stilled, expecting her to thrust him away.

She didn't.

She eased closer to him and he rejoiced silently at the victory. It was a huge step forward for them and whatever had been happening between them. It also gave him his first real feel of her. She was too thin. The woman needed to eat more. He liked his females with meat upon their bones. He caressed her hip gently.

"Yes," responded Rossi, his gaze keen as he questioned her knowledge of him with his eyes rather than his mouth. "I'm the youngest."

"Your poor mother," she said to Keonae. "You're hardly a small guy and Rossi is nearly as big as you. Tell me you were all tiny babies at least or I'm going to feel horrible for her."

Keonae hid his smile. "Actually, we were not that small, considering."

"Seriously?"

"Yes."

"Oh dear, that poor woman." Her fingers twirled the ends of his hair in the back. The action felt so natural, as if she'd done that very thing to him hundreds of times before. Yet, this was her first, but he hoped not her last. "I still can't believe she had that many multiples without the aid of fertility drugs."

"Yeah." He caressed her hip more, wanting to ease his hand down and over her backside. Hers was a bottom begging to be touched. "It's certainly something."

"And you," she said to Lazar. "You're the friend from out of town who he's known a few years now?"

Out of town? More like a rival kingdom.

Lazar offered a suave smile. "I am."

"Congrats on your marriage."

Lazar lifted one brow, his gaze finding Keonae. Keonae knew the man wondered how much Lark actually knew about them. "Thank you," he said to Lark, though he continued to hold Keonae's gaze.

"Then you must be the childhood friend," she said to Sachin. "I enjoy hearing stories about the trouble you'd all get in, even though Keonae is kind of cryptic at times. But still, they're amusing. It's nice to meet you all. He talks about you all so much I feel like I kind of know you." She smiled at Sachin. "You're the one with the little girls, right?"

A guarded look moved over Sachin's face. Keonae knew why. He was protective of his family. None could blame him. "I am."

"They're adorable. Keon has shown me some pictures of them along with his nephews. I'm not sure what's in the water in your hometown, but you all sure have a run on twins and more."

"Perhaps," Sachin leveled his silver gaze on her, a knowing smile creeping onto his face, "you will find yourself having a set as well if you and Keonae act on the feelings you appear to have for one another."

Keonae jerked, accidentally whacking his knee on the table leg and bumping Lark. She fell and he caught her, dragging her onto his lap with one hand and steadying her tray of beers with the other.

She set them on the table and remained on his lap. There was no masking his body's reaction to her. She had to feel his erection through his jeans for it was pressed against her ass.

"P-perhaps," she said, making his throat go dry.

Keonae grabbed a beer and chugged it, ignoring Sachin's chuckle. He kept an arm firmly planted around Lark's waist, wanting her to remain upon his lap a while longer. He'd wanted to have her this close for a month, from the moment he'd laid eyes upon her.

"Though, all joking aside," she said, facing forward, but leaning against him. "Multiples do kind of run in my family too."

Rossi laughed snidely. "Having them run in your family is very different from being one." Rossi muttered something under his breath about stupid humans and Sachin growled from across the table.

"And you know so much of this?" Keonae asked Rossi, his temper waning.

Rossi grumbled, his mood foul as he

spoiled for a fight. One Keonae would soon give him at the rate he was going.

Sachin grabbed the beers and thrust one at Rossi, grunting. "Drink, it will keep your mouth occupied and mayhap keep nonsense from falling free of your lips."

Lark remained on his lap and he took the chance to take in the peach scent from her hair. He tightened his hold on her, wanting the clothing between them to be no more. He'd fantasized about having her on him. Having her ride him while she took him deep and hard.

"Oh, I'm well aware of what it's like to be a twin. There is a bond there that is really indescribable," she said, loneliness in her voice.

"Read that in a book?" his brother questioned, continuing to be as big of an ass as he could be. As soon as Lark was free from his line of sight, Keonae planned to level his brother. It was high time someone put Rossi in his place. He was far too pampered for Keonae's liking.

"Brother, I know not what has gotten

into you, but continue and I will beat it out of you."

"He is not sleeping," said Sachin. "Worry for his woman keeps him awake and in the foulest of moods. Consider not killing on this evening. Perhaps on the morrow."

Keonae glared at Rossi. It was hard to give his brother the benefit of the doubt when it was Lark he was being rude to. Any other and he might forgive it, but not her.

Lark took a deep breath. "I was a twin."

Keonae stroked her back lightly, surprised to hear her confess to having a twin. "You never told me you have a twin."

She tensed. "Because I don't."

Confused, he continued to touch her. "But you just said you—"

"She passed away a little over thirteen years ago." She patted his leg and tried to stand. "Enough talk of it."

Keonae tugged on her, forcing her to lean back against him more. She did and he put his chin on her shoulder. It was a position he'd seen human lovers in bars assume on more than one occasion, though it was a first for him. "You could have told me that before. I'd have avoided talking about my brothers."

Her hand came to the side of his face with the scar. He flinched, but she kept her hand there. She did a semi hug-like move, their heads touching. "I like hearing about them. And I should get up and work, not sit on my backside."

"I disagree." He resisted the urge to kiss her cheek. "I think you're fine right here."

"I'm not sure my boss would agree."

"Then quit and let me take care of you." The words left his mouth before his head could catch up to them. When his brain landed on what he'd said, he tensed, but decided against taking it back. He had more money than he knew what to do with. She didn't need to work and he desperately wanted more time with her.

She'll hurt you.

She laughed. "Right. Would that make

you my sugar daddy? No. I think you'd have to be much older than you are."

If she only knew.

He grinned and then nipped at her palm, moving it from his face, thankful she'd not touched his scars directly. "I'm older than I look."

Chapter Four

LARK SIGHED AND TURNED HER FACE enough that her forehead touched Keonae's cheek as her stomach knotted. He was a complication she couldn't afford. She should have been on her way already.

Never plant roots for more than a few months.

The bad guys always managed to find her if she did. But she couldn't leave Keonae. Couldn't just vanish. He'd become important to her in ways he couldn't possibly realize. She felt something for him. Something more than she was willing to state out loud. And something more than he probably felt for her.

She smiled, enjoying the closeness he was permitting her. He was usually so standoffish, always avoiding looking at her directly or encouraging any sort of real contact.

As much as she knew she should stay removed from people and keep her distance for their own safety—she had her own demons, except hers pursued her in real life instead of her dreams. She desired him and the comfort he provided. Hers was a lonely existence and he had filled a void for her. Getting close to him and sharing anything real about her past was beyond foolish, yet she'd found herself doing so again and again with him. Life on the run certainly wasn't an easy one. Keonae made it at least bearable. Even from the moment they first met he'd helped her without realizing as much.

He was quiet, at first often listening more than he contributed in the way of conversation. Gradually, that had changed, and he'd opened up more and more to her, though still guarded. Most days he showed up an hour or so after she arrived and stayed until closing, before going with her to the twenty-four-hour diner down the road. She enjoyed the company. As much as she pushed him to be around other people because of how alone he was, she wasn't much better. He was her only friend.

The guy had a badass-biker vibe. Plus, he rode a big motorcycle that roared so loud there was no mistaking it was him. Every ounce of him was ripped to the point she had a hard time tearing her gaze from him. Come to think of it, all the men at the table were built in that manner.

Lark rubbed his forearm gently, marveling at his body as she did. His friends razzed him about various things, mostly the motorcycle he owned. They seemed to get a kick out of it, although she wasn't sure why. All she knew was that she liked touching him and being near him. He made her feel safe.

Groaning, she stood, not wanting to get back to work, but knowing she needed to. Keonae's hand skimmed her ass and excitement raced through her. He tugged on her, dragging her back to the spot on his lap. Damn, the man felt good.

Too good.

She'd often lain in bed, thinking of what it would be like to have him above her. To have him buried deep in her. Every time she pictured it, she rubbed herself and came long and hard. The man screamed sex appeal. Just the thought made her body tingle.

"Sit and stay," he pleaded. He'd never asked her to remain near him before, and she had to admit she liked hearing him voice his yearning to keep her closer to him.

She bent and kissed his cheek with the scar on it. He tensed and she remained there, making a point to kiss the scar itself. "Thank you for giving me something to look forward to every night."

The expression on his face was unreadable.

She put her lips to his ear. "Did I do something wrong?"

"No," he returned tersely.

"I need to get back to work. I'll leave you all to enjoy yourselves."

He stiffened. "Stay."

She glanced past him at his friends and brother. They were all gawking at them. Uneasy, Lark wiggled on Keonae's lap, drawing a gasp from him in the process. "I said something that upset you."

Bewilderment coated his expression. "No."

"I saw you shut down on me," she confessed, glancing away.

He took hold of her wrists, moving her hands from his face. He kissed her palms. "My demons are showing through. You did nothing."

It hit her then. He'd shut down on her when she'd kissed his scar. Her jaw set and she freed her hands from his grasp, placing her fingers on his cheek once more. He flinched, confirming her suspicions. With deliberate slowness, Lark eased closer, her lips finding his scars once more. She planted a row of tiny kisses upon them and then kissed his lips chastely, despite wanting more.

When Keonae tensed to the point he was stiff as a board beneath her, she leaned more, putting her lips to his ear. "You are so fucking sexy."

His breath caught and his fingers dug deep into her hips. "L-Lark?"

"I don't want to get up. I want to sit here and kiss every inch of you, Keon," she whispered.

He ran a hand up her back.

"Nothing to say to that?" she asked.

He appeared to be at a total loss for words. "Yes?"

She laughed.

"Do I get to kiss you back then?"

She wanted to ravish the man. What girl wouldn't? "Deal."

With that, she stepped away from him just as a few stragglers came into the pool-room area, and it was easy to see they were going to be a rowdy crowd. Not only that, she'd been told by the owner the back pool area was off limits to everyone but Keonae and his buddies. She didn't question why.

"Hey now, look at that," one of the guys said, sounding as if he had showed up drunk. He lifted a pool stick. "Bobby, check her out, man. She's fucking hot."

"Keonae, leave it be," one of the men at Keonae's table said. "They are intoxicated. Nothing more."

Suddenly, strong hands were on her hips. She gasped as warmth spread through her. Leaning back, she settled against the wall of muscle behind her, catching the scent of Keonae. Just being near him made her body quiver.

The frat boys snickered, showcasing their immaturity and stupidity. "Oh, look out, Ray, or the big bad boyfriend will threaten to kick your ass."

"Actually," Lazar said. "He will not bother with a threat. I am fairly sure Keonae will simply kill you."

Whatever the frat boys saw made them glance nervously at each other and then start into a game of pool as if they'd not just gone out of their way to be total dickheads.

Lark tried to turn to face Keonae, but

he held her in place. "Why don't you go ahead into the main part of the bar, Lark?"

She put her hand over his and caressed it gently. "Because you want to get into a fight without me in here to see it?"

"Yes."

She laughed softly. "At least you're honest. But, Keon, I don't need you to get into a bar fight over me. I get by fine on my own. Thank you, though. The gesture was nice."

"Did someone actually refer to Keonae as nice?" Keonae's brother said from the table behind them.

"Shut up, Rossi," Keonae said, keeping his hand on her shoulder.

She used the moment to twist and face him. He was breathtaking. His squared jawline and hard features combined with jet-black hair that hung just past his shoulders and golden eyes were oddly familiar. Her womanly parts screamed at her to jump his bones, that he'd be the best she ever had and then some. Whatever the man had going on, her ovaries were totally weak to it. They were bordering on begging.

Hurt flashed in his eyes as her hand found his left cheek. Scars ran down the entire left side of his face, starting somewhere up and under the do-rag he wore. She'd caught sight of others in their time together. Some ran from his hands up his forearms, deeper on one arm than the other, and she knew he had some on one side of his neck as well. She'd never seen him shirtless, but her guess was, he was scarred under there as well. It didn't matter to her. Even with the scars he was gorgeous. In fact, they somehow added to his appeal.

They told a story. They said he'd been through something horrible and come out the other side of it. She had scars too. Some on the outside; most on the inside. All of them had a story of their own, but combined to make her the person she was today.

He attempted to jerk away from her

touch, but she put her other hand on his steely chest, her lips curving upward. "Hi."

His brows met. "Hi?"

Lark grinned.

Slowly but surely, Keonae did as well. His smile was barely there but a smile all the same.

"Keonae," Rossi said, sounding annoyed. Lark got the feeling Rossi didn't want his brother to have anything to do with her. She'd have taken offense, but Rossi's instincts were spot on. She was nothing but trouble. She knew it. Keonae would learn it soon enough if he stuck around that long.

"You can wait a moment, brother." Keonae's hands came up and over hers.

Rossi snorted. "Or you could get your ass over here and discuss what we traveled here to talk to you about."

His brother wasn't as funny and nice as Keonae had described him, but he had a point. They'd come far to see him and she was monopolizing his time. She separated from Keonae and put a bit of distance between them. "Go talk with them. You told me they don't live close. He's right. Kind of a dick, but right."

"Lark," Keonae said, his voice deep and only slightly accented compared to the thicker ones his friends and brother had. She could listen to him talk all day and night. From the second they met, she'd wanted him in a way that wasn't natural. She wasn't the type of girl who could dare want anything more than a night of pleasure from a man. She couldn't commit to one and she certainly couldn't do long term.

Not if she wanted to keep her secret.

Get some distance now.

She hurried out of the back room and checked the other tables to see if anyone needed anything.

A half-hour ticked by and Lark headed to the back area with more beers. She set them on the corner of their table, keeping her gaze lowered from Keonae and his friends as she collected their empty bottles.

Keonae moved closer to her, his hand

finding her arm. Her head screamed for distance again, but her traitorous body cozied up against him, her eyes closing a moment as she enjoyed his warmth.

"Getting to spend time with your brother?"

"I am. I would like to apologize for his behavior. This is out of character for him, I assure you," he said, so formal yet so full of concern, she melted. He slinked his hands up her sides, making her breath catch. She'd wanted him to make this much contact with her from day one, but he'd been so standoffish, so closed off from physical contact that she'd nearly given up. Having his friends and family near him did him wonders.

"I have to clean up."

"You do not," he said. "I will make the little men clean up after themselves." He glanced at the frat boys and she nearly laughed at his use of little men.

She patted Keonae's chest. "I'll just do it. Less drama."

"I dislike you waiting on them."

She wasn't proud of her job, but it paid

the bills and gave her a roof over her head. She pulled away from him, wanting a bit of space. She threw away the empty bottles left sitting around the back room. The frat boys were good and soaked now. Two were using one another for support to stay upright. She approached with caution. "You guys want me to call a cab for you?"

"Mmm," Bobby hummed, his gaze going to her crotch. "I've got something on my mind that you can do, but it's not call us a cab."

"Keonae, sit," Rossi said. "You are on the verge of losing control and I have not the care to deal with this on this evening."

"Brother," Keonae warned.

"Think the bitch gets off on brother action?" another one of the frat boys asked. At the rate he was going, Lark was going to be left no choice but to handle him and his buddies. So much for hoping they'd simply drink their fill and leave well enough alone.

"We can see how she likes more than one man in her at time," Ray said.

Lark put a hand up, stopping Keonae,

already knowing he'd do something if she didn't. She focused on the frat boys. "You should leave now. Take the offer of a cab. If you don't—"

"What?" Bobby asked, his chest puffing as thoughts of being a badass danced through his head. "You gonna take your boy off his leash?"

Lark smiled, knowing it was anything but kind or friendly. "He should be the least of your concerns. Now take the offer and go peacefully. Please."

They laughed.

Never a good sign.

Clearly, too much to drink had left them with an over-inflated belief in their abilities, because from where she was standing, Keonae could wipe the floor with them. Not that she needed him to. She was capable of doing it all by her lonesome.

Keonae moved past her and went at the first guy. She called out to him, but he didn't even register her as being there. He was fixated on the frat boys. Lark stood there totally dumbfounded as the gentle giant she'd come to love conversing with seized hold of one of the frat boys and lifted him by the throat with one hand. The boy's feet dangled off the ground and Keonae didn't look the least bit strained. In truth, he appeared to be holding back.

She gasped.

Her giant was apparently far from gentle.

Very far from it.

"Keonae?"

He paid her no mind, lifting the boy higher off the ground. Keonae's friends advanced on him, yanking him back from the boy, freeing the kid in the process. The boy fell to the floor with a thud and no one seemed to much care as he fought for air, his eyes wide as he rubbed his neck before wisely running off with the others.

Lazar motioned for Lark to come closer to Keonae. "You calm him down. He will not hit you. Us, he'll pummel until we are nothing more than ground-up bits."

She nearly protested, but the expression on Keonae's face said Lazar was right. He'd beat the crap out of his friends if they tried to get near him in his current state of mind. Which was apparently superhero, pissed-off mode. He rolled his head, his neck cracking loudly, the muscles in his upper body straining from his clear need to hit something. Whatever was unlucky enough to be the target wouldn't survive. From the way he was standing and the power rolling off him in waves, he wasn't to be messed with. Such a change from the quiet biker she'd come to think she knew.

"Keon?"

He didn't respond. Though he did stop tensing his upper body.

Lazar lifted his hand to her again. "Come. He won't harm you."

She did as instructed, slipping past Rossi and pressing herself to Keonae. She smoothed her hands over his chest and then cupped his face. He grabbed her right wrist and tried to pull her hand from his scars. She went to her tiptoes. "Is this why you duck away when I'm around, or do I just repulse you?"

"Repulse me?" he asked, sounding

flabbergasted. "You? Repulse me? Not possible."

It was hard to hide her excitement in knowing he was attracted to her as well. "Then I'll take that answer to mean you think you need to hide from me. Why?"

The look he gave her was telling. He did want to hide his scars from her.

Stupid man.

"Keon, I've been waiting for nearly a month for you to man up and ask me out on a real date instead of ordering me to eat breakfast with you, and all this time you've been too chicken to?"

His friends laughed.

"She just called him a chicken," one said.

"Wrong bird," Lazar said, coughing as he laughed.

She didn't get the joke, nor why it seemed so funny to the men with Keonae.

Keonae tipped his head.

"Well?" Lark pinched at his washboard abs to no avail. "Are you going to ask me out now or do I have to ask you?"

"Um, yes?"

Even his brother laughed at his response.

Lark smiled wide. "And can you do me a favor and stop hiding yourself? I very much like looking at *all* of you."

Chapter Five

KEONAE FOUGHT FOR WORDS, BUT coherent thoughts and the ability to speak had started to fail him somewhere around the time the little human males began their taunting of Lark. Memories best left in the past had surfaced, leaving him wanting to kill every male present to protect her. While he'd realized he'd not actually loved the woman he'd been betrothed to long ago, he'd never wanted her to meet such an ugly fate as the one she'd been dealt. It didn't matter what he said to his friends. Truth was, it had been hard to witness the aftermath of what the falcons and the vultures had done to her, regardless of her betrayal.

When the humans had threatened Lark, something in him snapped. He wouldn't tolerate one hair upon her golden head being harmed. It was irrational and he knew it. He had wanted to shout "mine" and claim her then and there for all around him to see, but that made little sense to him. He'd been around her for nearly a month, and while he did want to be near her, he'd never had to fight to keep from outright laying claim to her. Seeing the little humans think they could touch her had driven him over the edge of reason.

Was his mind broken as well as his body?

Take her. Claim her.

He growled, his gaze finding her.

Claim her. She is yours.

He knew it deep down, but denial won out. He had spent so long believing he'd live a life of solitude, a life without a mate, without the chance of a family, that to accept it at a moment's notice was simply too much. And there was Lark to think about. She deserved more than him. On top of that, even, he was not human. How did he go about telling her that he wanted to make her his mate and that he had wings?

That was not an easy topic to approach with anyone, let alone the woman who stirred things in him he'd assumed long dead.

Her thumb traced over the bottom portion of the scars on his face. It was strange to have someone touching them. Most people shied away from them. The women he'd bedded over the years never made any attempt to make contact with his face. He put them on their hands and knees and fucked them from behind—nice and impersonal. The way he preferred it.

Maybe he'd put too long between sexual escapades. Perhaps that was why he was so drawn to Lark. Maybe if he found another human woman who held little appeal to him, he could fuck her and gain some semblance of control around Lark.

Pfft. Doubtful.

Lark was different. When she'd first caught a glimpse of what he'd done his best to hide, he'd assumed she was repulsed. The strange look of lust and wonder that came over her beautiful face still took him by surprise. Besides, the idea of touching another woman turned his stomach.

Mayhap his mind was broken.

His body certainly seemed to be.

Her body was pressed against his and his cock hardened to the point he worried it might actually work its way out of the top of his jeans. Lark rubbed against him and stilled, her mouth forming an "O". She blushed and he knew then she felt his erection, felt what she did to him.

Grinning, he managed to find his voice, thankful it hadn't up and totally abandoned him. His friends and brother would never let him live it down if he clammed up around a woman. "Can I please beat the tiny men to a bloody pulp?"

"No," she responded evenly.

"I would very much like to ask you out."

"Ask her out?" Sachin questioned. "He sounds so very local. Does he not?"

"Sachin, don't make me add you to the list of ass-kickings I'll be delivering," Keonae stated, a slight teasing note to his voice.

The next thing Keonae knew, Lark was pressing a chaste kiss to his lips and pinching his chin between her forefinger and thumb before giggling as she hurried off into the main portion of the bar. He stood rooted in place, watching her rush away. Every ounce of him demanded he go to her, toss her down, say the words his people said during a claiming ritual and mark her as his own.

His wife.

His chosen one.

"Is it me or does that beautiful woman seem to be totally taken with Keonae?" Sachin asked. "I am unsure why any woman would find him appealing. His personality leaves much to be desired."

Keonae glanced at his friend, grinning like a fledgling. His chest felt fluttery as if butterflies had taken up occupancy within it.

"If he begins skipping about the bar, can we tell everyone?" Rossi smiled.

It was good to see his brother coming on board with the jovial mood.

Keonae pointed at Rossi, leveling a menacing stare at him. "You have been most unpleasant on this night, little brother. You will tell my woman you are sorry or I will skin you alive. Understood?"

"Your woman?" asked Rossi.

"You should go with *yes*," Sachin said to Rossi before coming to Keonae and giving him a manly version of a hug. Large scale showing of affection wasn't common practice among their kind, and while it was appreciated, it was slightly awkward. "It is good to see you take a real interest in a woman again. If you have need of Paige or Rayna to assist in helping you to better understand human females, say the word and I will arrange for them to pay you a visit. You should be warned, Rayna's mood is most foul now that Kabril has impregnated her again. I believe the triplets were more than enough for her, but you know your brother, he wishes for a castle full of little ones."

"Speaking of little ones," Rossi said, a question hanging in the air. "Will Paige threaten my manhood if I get you home late tonight? She mentioned something about the girls being difficult."

"They are going through a rough stage," Sachin said with pride.

Keonae laughed. "Never did I think I'd be standing in a room with you all talking about kid stuff. Where are the fierce warriors I remember?"

"One too many diaper changes later and they are nearly nursemaids," Lazar said with a grin. He was to be a father before too long and looked to be longing for the very thing he just jested with the others about. "I hope none of you think to start trying to coddle me as a mother would. Your nurturing is leaking off you in waves."

"Rossi is the hugger of the group," added Sachin.

"Said the man who just hugged my brother," reminded Rossi.

"Watch how much you drink," Lazar noted as he nodded in Rossi's direction. "I've no wish to assist you while you are trying to fly drunk again. Your woman will skin me alive if I bring you home in that condition."

"Gentlemen," Sachin said. "I believe we can adjourn this meeting. Keonae has much more pressing matters at hand." The man's attention went toward the doorway that led to the front of the bar.

"Like bedding that beautiful woman who can see past his rather bad temper," Lazar stressed.

"A game of pool before we call it a night?" Rossi asked. "I love my woman to death, but she is scary as can be right now. I'd like to postpone my demise."

"Sure."

Chapter Six

LARK PUT AWAY THE LAST OF THE GLASSES and nodded to the bartender who notified everyone it was last call. Some patrons grumbled, but all knew the bar was closing soon enough. "Lenny, I can finish up with closing," she said.

The bartender faced her. "You sure you don't mind?"

"I know you have a big job interview in the morning. Go on. I've got this."

He left and she continued on with what needed done to finish out the night. She headed into the back room to find Keonae and his friends at a pool table, still drinking. The men seemed to be able to put the beer away without noticing or showing the effects.

Keonae looked up and scratched his shot as she entered.

Laughing, Lazar raised his beer to her. "My thanks. He was going to wipe the floor with me until the sight of you threw him off his game."

She blushed and bit at her lower lip. "I do what I can to help out."

Keonae approached her, discarding his pool stick in an ungraceful fashion. It missed the other table and landed with a sharp crack on the floor. Keonae paid little mind to it.

Rossi snorted. "I believe he wishes to take you to his home and bed you."

Keonae snarled and Lark grabbed his wrist.

"Okay." It was stupid to offer herself up and she knew it. Taking him home with her wouldn't end with one night. Deep down she was aware of as much, but she couldn't seem to stop herself. She wanted him desperately. Normally, she spent at least a few months in one location, but she hadn't planned on Keonae, on how much she'd want him. She'd bed him and then cut out of town come morning. It was the only safe thing to do. She would bring nothing but death and destruction into his life. He didn't need that, and she couldn't live with herself if anything happened to him because of her.

His head whipped around. "What?"

She smiled. "I said okay. I'm game if you are."

He blinked in disbelief.

"Old friend," Sachin said, clasping onto Keonae's shoulder. "The woman agreed to go home with you and permit you to pleasure her. What are you doing standing here with us? Change your mind on the coddling?"

Impudently, Lark slipped her hand into Keonae's. "Yes, what are you doing standing here with them?"

"Lark?" He caressed her inner wrist.

Awareness prickled along her skin with each swipe of his finger. His palm was callused, yet she very much wanted it running all over her body. Everything about the man turned her on.

He leaned in, putting his mouth to her ear. "Teasing me would be a bad thing, Lark. I'm not a man who can pull back once I start something."

"Funny," she commented. "I've been wondering if you're the type of guy who ever starts anything."

"Oh, I will start something, all right." His lips brushed her ear and she sank against him. The man could make her melt with just the hint of more to come. "Are you done for the night?"

"Almost. Last call was just issued. Are we still going to breakfast together?" She enjoyed their morning ritual, but had to admit she was all for skipping it and getting straight to the fucking-like-bunnies part of the night. She raked her gaze over his form. There wasn't an ounce of fat on him. Sheer perfection, and he would be in her soon enough. Her panties moistened.

"It would be wise," he said, nibbling on her earlobe. "You'll need all the energy you can get for when I take you home with me."

"We're really doing this then?"

He nodded and drew her closer, rubbing against her like a cat, his body hard all over. She moaned softly and he laughed, the sound deep and full of manly pride. "Oh, we are most certainly doing this."

She cupped his face, loving touching him. "I really love this new you. Your friends and brother bring out a side of you that I can't wait to explore."

"My sweet, you will see every side of me soon enough."

"Promise?" she asked, liking the way he spoke.

He dragged a hand through the back of her hair as he kissed her neck. "You have my word."

A languorous smile moved across her face. Realizing she was practically fawning over the man while they had an audience, she composed herself. His friends returned to their table with beers in hand. Keonae swatted her backside playfully before joining them.

Lark took her time cleaning up the back room, enjoying being near Keonae and his friends. She hadn't been able to have anyone close to her for long, so friends weren't an option for her and she had no family left to speak of. She filled her tray full of empty bottles, and Keonae turned and tried to take it from her.

"I've got it," she said.

He scowled. "I dislike how hard you have to work."

Sachin approached, pool stick in hand, the men having started another game at some point. "Hmm, if only a prince would come along and sweep her off her feet."

Keonae lifted a middle finger and held it up, never moving from her side.

"I have a wife who does that for me," said Sachin. "She is far better looking than you, old friend."

Lark laughed. "Keon, let him be. I'm not into princes and fairy tales anyway. I'm more based in reality. You know, where you're hard-pressed to get a guy to phone you back come the next morning."

Sachin paused. "I suspect you will have no issues getting him to return your calls."

Lazar stepped closer. "The problem may be getting him to leave you alone."

Rossi snorted.

Keonae groaned. "See why I rarely allow them around people?"

She winked. "I think they're great."

"The more you get to know them, the more your attitude will change. They are like boils on the asses of all around them."

She broke into a fit of laughter and pressed tighter to him. She knew he had a funny side. He'd shown it to her on occasion. It was rare but there. "Boils on the butts, huh?"

"Most certainly."

His brother shook his head. "Keeping it sophisticated, I see."

Keonae flipped him off as well.

Lark hadn't felt this happy, this light and free from her worries, in years. She twisted against Keonae, unable to hide her joy any longer. She wrapped her arms around his neck and went to her tiptoes, her lips meeting his. The kiss wasn't chaste but remained this side of too dirty. That didn't stop need from slamming into her. She wanted him fiercely.

She drew back, her gaze moving over a shocked Keonae. She touched his lower lip. "I have a few things left to do to help close up and then we can blow this Popsicle stand."

His brows met. "They sell frozen treats on a stick here? It seems an odd choice for such an establishment."

She paused and then laughed at his odd sense of humor. "Sometimes I'd swear you were born on another planet."

"No. Not another planet." His expression turned guarded as he caressed her cheek. "Hurry with whatever you must do."

"I will." She darted away, knowing if she didn't make a clean break from him right then and there, she might never. Her common sense told her to keep going, run right out the front door of the bar and don't look back. That she'd bring a mountain of trouble to him—the kind he wouldn't walk away from, no matter what kind of badass biker dude he was.

The things of nightmares sought her out. They weren't human. They didn't leave witnesses, and they were ruthless. She'd managed to dodge them for the past few months, staying on the move, but deep down she got the sense they were close on her heels. And she knew if she dared to stay on much longer, she'd fall for Keonae and might never leave.

You've already fallen for him.

She tried to make a move for the door, but her gut clenched, heat racing over her as nausea rose quickly. Her entire body racked with pain and she whimpered, unsure what was happening to her.

Warm, strong arms wrapped around her waist, drawing her back against a frame she had already come to recognize as Keonae's. The pain, the wave of sickness, all of it washed away from her almost instantaneously with his touch.

He put his mouth to her ear. "Who threatened you?"

"W-what?" she questioned, her mind unable to follow as her body sparked with desire for him. She might burn alive if he didn't make love to her and soon.

"I felt your fear, your pain," he said, his voice low, deep, menacing, yet she didn't fear him. He'd never harm her. She knew that deep in her bones. Another sure fact hit her—he would have her and she would never be the same. Neither would he.

She was a mess he didn't need. The darkness that followed her around would catch up to her. It always did, and Keonae would be in its crosshairs. She didn't want that.

Didn't want him hurt. Not because she couldn't control the magnetic pull to him. She couldn't seem to get one foot to move in front of the other so that she could step out of his grasp. He felt so good. So right.

Running her hands over his arms, Lark closed her eyes briefly, enjoying his touch. She couldn't remember a time when she'd allowed another to comfort her in such a way. "No one threatened me."

"But I felt your pain."

Felt my pain?

She turned her head, looking over her shoulder at him, and he eased a hand up, just under her left breast. Her nipples tightened to diamond-like points and she shook with wanton desire for him. She'd managed to control her attraction to him for nearly a month. Why was she suddenly having issues?

Stop touching him.

Hell, stop being touched by him.

Her body ignored her mind's ravings. It wanted him to touch her more intimately and it wanted less clothing between them. She writhed against his form, the feel of his erection digging at her backside. A growl of masculine triumph came from him and she bent her head awkwardly, unconcerned with how uncomfortable the action was.

His lips grazed hers and fire shot through her body, giving her the answers she'd sought. The reason why she was having such a hard time resisting him all of a sudden. As her gaze eased over his lips, it all became crystal clear. They'd kissed and it had apparently weakened her resolve to him. For some reason, the action had left her a mind-numbed sex addict with a singular focus.

Him.

"Keonae?" asked Sachin, his voice off. "Is all well?"

Keonae jerked her tighter against his frame. "She is trying to make me believe so, yet I felt her pain, old friend. I felt her fear as if it were my own."

Lark tried to focus on what he was saying, but she couldn't, not with him touching her. Stirrings of lust guided her actions as she continued to rub her body against his. It was animalistic and she couldn't find it in herself to care. She laid her head back against him, noticing how perfectly they fit together. It was as if they were made for one another.

He jerked her tight to him, his hips thrusting against her backside, leaving no room for doubt. He was as turned on as she was. And nothing on the man was small by anyone's standards.

She gulped.

He growled again, nipping at her ear. "I want to be in you, *ta'konima*."

The men all sounded shocked by whatever Keonae had just said to her. She was too caught up in the lust to pay it much mind.

"Oh shit," said Rossi, his voice barely there. "This is big. What do we do?"

"For now, assure he does not do anything foolish," said Lazar. "He is still being driven by testosterone from the human boys threatening her. In this state, he could cause her harm without meaning to."

"I vote you grab him," said Rossi, a note of concern in his voice. "I like my body parts attached."

"Ever the brave one," said Lazar mockingly.

Sachin stepped closer and Lark became vaguely aware that Lazar and Rossi were on the other side, as if they were all flanking Keonae, preparing to do battle of some sort.

Sachin lifted his hands. "Keonae, look at me. I believe mating heat as well as warrior ways of old have you in their grasp."

"This is not good," said Rossi, clucking his tongue. "Not good at all."

"Give her to me slowly," pressed Sachin, his hands up. "We only wish to see to her safety."

Keonae growled and she understood the warning he was giving his friends. If they tried to take her from him, he'd react with violence. He'd already shown her there was far more to him than she'd thought. Her mild-mannered biker had a temper and the juice to back it up. There had been enough violence already. No more needed to occur. Not over her.

She turned in his arms, his hand twisting her t-shirt as she went. She touched the sides of his face. "Keonae?"

He trembled under her touch. "Who threatened you, *ta'konima*?"

"Ta whata?" she questioned, unable to look away from his penetrating gaze.

"I stand by my first oh shit," said Rossi.

"Now who sounds local?" asked Sachin.

Rossi grunted. "Is she *his*?"

Lazar stepped closer, lifting his hands in a sign he meant no harm. "I would say so, yes."

Keonae squeezed her tighter to him.

She gasped. He was hurting her, but he shouldn't have been able to. She wasn't like other women. No. Far from it. "Stop coming closer. You're making him worse."

The men froze.

"Keonae, you're hurting me."

His grip was iron-clad. She tried to pry free, but that only served to make him tighten his already tight grip.

"Ouch."

His gaze snapped to her and he blinked, coming out of whatever hold he'd been under. He released her quickly and took a step back. "Lark, I didn't mean to."

She remained in place, watching him closer, a sinking feeling coming over her. He shouldn't have been able to keep her in place. He shouldn't have been able to inflict pain on her. Yet he'd done both with ease. The only people in her life who could do something similar weren't really people at all. They were monsters. "*How* did you hurt me?"

Puzzled, he simply stared at her. "I held you too tightly."

"That isn't what I meant," she said, easing closer to him. She looked him up and down, noting his size, how incredibly fit he was—how fit they all were. It was there, niggling at the back of her mind, so close yet just out of reach for her.

Think, Lark.

All of her instincts kicked in and the hair on the back of her neck rose as she began to put the pieces together at an alarming rate where she'd been blind to them before. She wasn't a fool. She knew there was more to the world than most humans understood. She knew very little was as it normally appeared to be, yet she'd had blinders on with Keonae for weeks. She'd let her pull to him outweigh her better judgment.

His inhuman strength, their accents, their ability to drink in such quantities without seeming affected in the least, and their sometimes strange speech patterns. Not to mention their size.

Giants.

How could she have missed it all when her life depended on her being alert? She'd never missed signs before. She always recognized the demons that hunted her.

Always.

But not with him.

Not with Keonae.

"I know *what* you did. What I don't understand is *how* you could hurt me. How did you have enough strength to cause me pain, Keonae? What are you? Are you something more than human?" she asked, desperate for him to dispel what she was fast beginning to believe was true.

He was one of them.

The bird men.

He shook his head. "I do not understand."

Lazar sniffed the air and gasped. "Smell. It is so faint it almost isn't there."

Sachin took a deep breath and his gaze snapped to her. "You are as we are? You are of the bird shifters?"

Lark's heart sank and she took a giant step back from them. She was an idiot and her stupidity would cost her life in the end. "I'm nothing like any of you."

She turned to run, but Keonae caught her, lifting her effortlessly, holding her to him. "Let go of me!"

"Lark?" he asked, sounding hurt and perplexed.

She didn't struggle, even though she knew she could put up a good fight. She'd done so many times in her life with the birdmen. How had she let him get so close to her? Why hadn't she noticed he was different? More to the point, why wasn't she terrified of him?

Why do I want him to fuck me?

Sachin eased closer slowly. "Old friend, she is as we are. Do you smell it on her? It is so faint I would have missed it had Lazar not caught it."

Rossi gasped. "Cursed Magaious, she's a shifter?"

"Yes, bring down the wrath of the bird gods upon us for taking their names in vain," snapped Sachin. "That is sure to make it all better."

"What? I slept on a hard stone floor, have had nearly no sleep, and my wife may or may not let me in our bed again because I impregnated her. To top off my day, I find out my brother's woman is a bird shifter masquerading as a human."

Keonae lifted her high off her feet. "She is no such thing. Stand back."

Sachin remained in place. He did his best to appear as though he was no threat. "We mean her no harm, Keonae. She is afraid *of us*. Do you sense that upon her?

"She was hurt and in pain," he said, sounding bewildered. His pain reached through her, as if it were hers, as he'd described happening to him on her account only moments before.

It broke her heart. He was no threat to her. She understood that. She lowered her head and confessed to him. "I was thinking of running away. Of taking off and leaving without telling you goodbye. The idea of leaving you hurt me, Keon. It made my body ache. You felt that. My fear of leaving you."

He tightened his hold on her and she whimpered. He released her and she faced him, seeing the hurt evident on his face. "You wished to run from me?"

"Maybe. I don't know," she said honestly. Her thoughts were scrambled. "I can't help the way I feel about you, and all of this was so intense all of a sudden. Then I started to worry about them finding me again and what they'd do to you." She snorted. "I didn't know you were one of them. You don't smell like them to me, so I didn't recognize it on you —and I think the little bits I did see, I chose to ignore because I'm attracted to you. I've never been attracted to one before. Ever. Normally, they make me want to vomit. They smell of death, evil, rotting flesh. They're monsters."

He just watched her, saying nothing, the pain still showing.

"What others?" asked Sachin.

"Perhaps my kind," said Lazar. "The

falcons have been known to be viewed as monsters."

She glanced at him. "No. You smell sweet to me. Almost *too* sweet, but sweet all the same. Well, not Keon. He doesn't smell sickly sweet to me. He smells perfect. They don't smell sweet at all. They smell like road kill. I'm not great with scents like they are. It takes me longer to smell things."

"I know not what roadkill is," said Sachin.

Rossi gasped. "She's talking about vultures. Lucy made the same comment when I came home after looking into a recent attack. I had engaged with a vulture, getting his blood on me, and upon my arrival home, Lucy said I smelled like roadkill to her."

All the men stepped closer to her, and Keonae didn't look like he was planning to attack them. He still looked hurt by her confession she'd been thinking of leaving him.

"Keonae, I thought about going, about taking off, but the minute I took one step toward that door with the intent of vanishing, everything on me hurt, and I thought I was going to be sick. You touched me then and it all went away."

Sachin rubbed his chin. "Your pull to him is great?"

She nodded.

"As is his to you," said Sachin, still worrying his jawline.

"True mates?" asked Lazar, sounding concerned.

Rossi nodded. "I'd wager yes. We could also consult the Oracle. Though, I have my suspicions it enjoys toying with us all."

She shook her head. "What are you all talking about?"

Sachin offered a reassuring look. "We believe you may be created for Keonae. His match in every way. The woman he is destined to be with. The woman he will sire children with."

Chapter Seven

KEONAE LOOKED UPON LARK, THE NEED to wrap his arms around her and spank her at war within him. How dare she think to run out on him! Did she not understand the pull he had to her? The craving he could not seem to sate?

He glanced to Sachin, thinking on what he'd said. Keonae's eyes widened. He took a giant step back. "She cannot be."

Sachin grinned. "We all suffer the same reaction, old friend. Denial simply wastes time you could be spent loving her. Would you rather not be in bed, filling her with your young ones?"

"You would be an expert on denying your feelings for your mate," said Rossi.

"And on little ones. You have how many now?"

Sachin offered a cross look.

Rossi laughed. "Hey, I'm not wrong."

No. He wasn't. Sachin had denied his feelings for his mate far longer than Keonae. None of that changed the fact that Lark could not be his mate.

"She is not my mate."

Lark crossed her arms over her chest and lifted a brow. There was no mistaking the clear offense she'd taken at his comments. "I may not understand everything going on here, but I have a feeling a true mate is someone special. Are you saying I'm not special?"

Rossi snorted. "Talk yourself out of this one, brother."

Keonae touched his scarred face. "She is stunning. She is a ray of light. She is good and pure. I am hideous. A monster with the taint of wars and death upon me. The bird gods would not shackle her to someone such as me. They would give her a man of honor, of means, of character."

Sachin rolled his eyes. "So you are

saying they would gift her a man who at great cost to himself fought to protect his kingdom, who is a prince by birth, wealthy beyond measure yet lives like he is poor, and a man who would lay down his life for those he loves?"

"Yes," said Keonae, reflecting. "That. They would give her that in a mate."

"He is describing you," Lazar said.

Keonae took another step back. "She is so beautiful. To be selected as my true mate and to get me—a hideous monster. I'm a beast and she's a beauty."

He yanked his shirt over his head, showing off his upper body, knowing the extent of the damage that had been done to him long ago by a group of vultures. They had taken turns clawing him open, dumping human soil into the wounds and then repeating the actions, before snapping his bones, laughing as his body fought to heal the damage but in the end failed.

He stared at Lark, wanting her to see how disgusting he was. He expected her to recoil in horror. The crazed woman licked her lips as if she was thinking of sliding closer and touching him.

Did she not see him?

"Holy crap, you're totally ripped," she said, her voice breathy. "You're the sexiest man I have ever seen."

His jaw set. Was she daft? "Look at me. *See* what is before you, woman."

"Oh, I'm a-looking all right," she said, biting her lower lip, nothing short of desire running over her face. "Can I touch what is in front of me? If I lick it, does it make it mine?"

Lazar barked with laughter at Lark's outburst.

Keonae tossed his hands in the air. "You are daft."

"Seems of sound mind to me," said Sachin. He eyed Keonae, having seen him more than once since the attack long ago without a shirt. "They are not as bad as they once were, old friend. But I believe your mind sees them as fresh as the day you received them. Not as they truly are."

Rossi had not seen Keonae shirtless since the attack. His brother neared him, pain in his gaze as he reached out to touch one of the many deep scars that traced Keonae's torso and back. He still remembered getting each one.

"Brother, this never healed beyond this point?" Rossi asked. "But we got you home and cleansed your wounds thoroughly."

Sachin drew Rossi back. "We were not quick enough, Rossi. He had been there for too long. The damage was permanent. And I do not speak falsehoods to your brother. The scars are not as severe as they once were."

"Brother," breathed Rossi, a tenderness to his voice that made Keonae uncomfortable. He did not want sorrow or remorse from his brother.

Keonae sighed. "Stop. I do not want your pity. I simply wish for you all to know why she is not for me. Why she cannot be my mate. She is perfection. I am all that is imperfect."

"You're a total dumbass," said Lark, surprising him.

He glanced to her.

She bit her lower lip. "If your stunt

was supposed to repulse me, you failed epically. All you did was turn me on more. I have big plans to lick every fucking inch of you, biker boy."

"Biker boy?" asked Lazar.

"Motorcycle man," Rossi added in explanation. "The machines with two wheels."

"Ah," said Lazar. "Yes, you have one of these?"

"I do," said Keonae.

"I wish to ride it."

"Another time, Lazar," said Sachin with a snort. "Let us convince him he is not a monster. Then you may ask to play with his human toys."

"You cannot convince me of such for I am a monster."

Lark's hands moved to her hips and the look she leveled upon him actually scared him. "Keon, if I hear you call yourself a monster again, I'm going to ram my boot so far up your ass that it won't ever come out. You are the single hottest man I've ever laid eyes on. You are super sexy. Do you know how many times

I've masturbated to images of you above me?"

She'd touched herself to thoughts of him? His cock sprang to life at the idea.

He stilled and then realized they weren't alone. "Did you have to say such a thing in front of them?"

Rossi laughed. "I changed my mind. I really like her. Claim her and let us all be on our way. I have relations to mend with my own woman. I have no wish to sleep upon a stone floor again."

Claim her?

The thought sent need pumping through him.

Lark continued to glare at him, cooling his passion. "Why do you see yourself as a monster? Because you have some scars?"

"*Some* scars?" he asked, there was very little of him that wasn't scarred in some fashion.

She turned her back to him and yanked off her shirt.

His cock threatened to burst free from his jeans at the sight of her bare back. *Cursed Magaious.* Did the woman have no mercy? Was she a sadist? Did she enjoy torturing him so? She would make one hell of a fine head of the dungeons back in Accipitridae. She was a master of cruel and unusual punishment, standing before him, teasing him in such a manner.

He would have grabbed her and fucked her had he not wanted her covered from the prying eyes of his friends and brother. Her naked form was for his eyes only. "Lark! Cover yourself. They are all mated, but to show them yourself is not acceptable."

"Brother," Rossi said softly. "She is showing you something that you do not see. Look."

He did, and slowly he began to see why she had exposed herself. The minute he spotted a row of scars that would line up perfectly to talons, rage coursed through him. The same fire that had burned in him long ago on the battlefield ignited. "Who hurt you? I will rip their heads off. I will tear them in two. I will dance upon their dissected corpses."

Lazar and Sachin grabbed him,

holding him in place as he continued to rant and rave. Lark was suddenly before him, her shirt back on. She touched his face.

"Stop."

He obeyed her instantly.

"I killed the man who did this to me," she said with a sigh. "But not before he killed my sister."

"The twin you spoke of," said Rossi.

She nodded.

"Who would dare to do such a thing?" asked Lazar. "Who would harm children? That is what you were when this happened, yes?"

She nodded and teared up. "He claimed to be our father. He said our mother was a human whore who had sold her body to his kind to be a birthing *chamber*, and that she'd hid us from him before abandoning us for being monsters. For being born from tests rather than a mated union. He said we had to go with him, that we had to fight in some war we'd never heard of. What I remember most was his smell. He smelled like death, like rotting flesh."

Sachin gasped. "Was your father of the vultures?"

She shrugged, loss on her face. "I don't know. He could shift into a bird, like the others who have come for me since then. I honestly didn't even know bird guys came in variety packs."

"Variety packs?" asked Sachin.

Rossi snorted. "Means different kinds."

Sachin lowered his gaze, somber. "Think she is the female we were told they seek?"

"They're always looking for me," said Lark softly. "This isn't something new."

Lazar shrugged. "Then we are wrong?"

Rossi glanced over Lark. "I smell it on you, but no offense, you don't seem very shifter like to me."

Lark inclined her head and then held up a hand. "Before you ask, I can't shift into a bird. I guess calling them vultures makes sense. Now that you say it, yes, I can see a resemblance in their wings when they're out. I can't believe I share DNA with a scavenger bird."

"You may not be of the vulture," said Sachin, hope in his voice. "It is possible you are of another line and that Rossi is mistaken."

Lark shifted from one foot to another. "If it helps any, I know my father's name. At least his first name. Cavanie. The ones who have come for me over the years talk about how I killed Cavanie."

Keonae sucked in a large breath. Cavanie was one of the vultures who had taken place in his torture. One of the evil vile men who had left Keonae scarred. The bastard was dead? And by Lark's own hands?

Sachin touched her and tried to pull her away from Keonae, worry in his eyes. "Come. It is wise you not be near him."

Keonae grabbed his friend, holding him in place. "You seek to take her from me?"

Rossi touched his arm. "Brother, he wishes to protect her from you."

"I would never hurt her."

Lazar sighed. "She just confessed to being fathered by a vulture. You hate their kind. You wish death upon them all. They are the reason you carry the scars. They are the reason you do not return to our realm."

Lark gasped and cupped her mouth.

Keonae charged past Sachin and grabbed her, drawing her close, kissing her forehead. He shook with raw hunger for her. "You did not do this to me. I do not hate you. I seek you out nightly in hopes of seeing you smile, of hearing your laugh, of being gifted the small bit of time and conversation you give me. I could never hate you. You make my body burn with need, my chest tight, and my thoughts a mess."

"You love her," said Rossi, appearing almost bored.

"Don't be ridiculous," said Lark, agitated. "He barely knows me."

Keonae lifted her gently, the emotions he'd fought so hard to deny surfacing quickly. "You are the reason I bother getting out of bed every day. You have given me something to look forward to. You give me purpose, Lark."

"You *love* her," stressed Rossi, smug satisfaction upon his face.

Keonae opened his mouth to object, but that wasn't what fell out. "Yes. I love her."

He practically leapt back, fearful he'd get it on him, whatever *it* was. Frantic, he glanced to Sachin for guidance—after all, the man was the king's adviser.

Sachin tipped his head back and laughed.

Some help he was.

Lark stared at him with wide eyes.

Rossi laughed too. "I've never seen him scared of anything. Now he's scared of a half-breed." His laughter faded as he commented. "I didn't mean it the wrong way. It's just that she smells mostly human to me with only slight undertones of shifter."

Keonae's jaw set. "Apologize to my woman this instant."

"Your woman?" asked Lazar as he licked his lips, hiding his amusement with the situation rather poorly. "The same woman you are about to take flight to run from?"

"Well, he is good at running," added Rossi, lifting his shoulders in casual reference. "Hey, it's true. He did take off and leave us all for how long? Ha, he's the prince of flight. Can we get that monogrammed on his ceremonial robes?"

"Your mood is less sour. This is good." Lazar scuffed Rossi on the back of the head and then dragged the man from Keonae's reach. "We shall go and let the two of you sort out this newfound connection for yourselves. You do not require witnesses."

Uneasy about being alone with Lark, because he did not trust himself not to ravish her, Keonae tried to go to Sachin who tossed his hands up and shook his head. "Oh no, old friend. You are on your own here. I will have guards sent this way to help you oversee the area. Before you protest"—he nodded in Lark's direction —"I suspect you will be quite busy with your new bride. Take the help, Keonae."

With that, the men exited the bar, leaving him standing there, afraid to face the one woman who had the power to bring him to his knees. She cleared her throat. He tried to pretend he didn't notice she wanted his attention.

"Really, you're going to act like you don't hear me? Are you also the prince of pre-school?" she demanded, tapping her foot.

He met her gaze.

She licked her lip. "You love me?"

"I do," he practically whispered.

"Why?"

He blinked. "You remind me of the sweet summers near the edges of the springs of the Tocalie Mountains. Your scent is like that of the mavabian flowers that dot the outer regions. I see you and every day I fight the urge to draw you close, to hold you, to join with you and most of all, to know you will never leave me."

She said nothing for a long moment and he realized what he'd done. He'd confessed love-sick nonsense to her and more than likely overwhelmed her with his clear state of need.

"Wow, that is not a line I've ever heard used before," she said with a slow smile. "I don't know anything about those mountains or that flower thing, but I have to say you won me over."

He nodded. "I was once known as a great romancer of women."

Her expression hardened. "Oh really?"

Keonae gulped, realizing too late that he'd said something he shouldn't have. Women raised in the human realm were quite confusing. A woman from his own realm would have been happy to hear he'd been sought after by many. Apparently, that did not translate over well to the human realm. "Did I say a great romancer of women? No. I lied."

"Uh-huh." She narrowed her gaze on him. "So you're really a prince of bird guys?"

He hid his laugh. "Yes, of the hawks of the realm."

"Realm?"

"You have much to learn of our kind,

Lark," he said, lifting his hand to her. He stared into her eyes, the attraction to her undeniable. She came to him willingly and he drew her in close, inhaling her scent, committing it to memory. Unable to hold back any longer, Keonae captured her lips with his, his tongue instantly finding hers. His scarred cheek pulled tight, but he didn't care. His only thoughts on her.

Chapter Eight

LARK RAN HER HANDS OVER ANY PART OF him she could reach. His scars felt silky smooth beneath her fingertips and she focused on them, knowing he needed a clear understanding that they didn't bother her. Far from it. The man was cut from the cloth of gods. The scars added to him, making him even sexier. She raked her nails over his back lightly as their kiss heated, the level of it growing to the point she moaned into his mouth.

His hands found her bra-covered breasts and he backed her up until she bumped a table and could go no more. He leaned and she eased onto the tabletop, thankful it was sturdy. Keonae continued to kiss her as he fondled her breasts through her bra. Wanting more, Lark grabbed for the tops of his jeans and opened them. She had only just skimmed her hand down the front of his pants when the door to the bar burst open, causing their kiss to end quickly.

"Keonae, help!"

It was Lazar and Rossi. They had another man with them who looked almost identical to Keonae, minus the scars. They held the man between them, their arms under his, aiding him in walking slowly. The man was covered in deep, bloody gashes. One hand was pressed to his side where it looked as though someone had attempted to disembowel him.

Sachin burst through the door behind them, a sword in hand as he yanked the door shut, locked it and he grabbed the handle with one hand. "Vultures."

The word caused fear to race up Lark's spine. They'd found her again.

Keonae gasped and struggled to button his jeans, stepping back from Lark, his attention on the newcomer. "Aeson? Brother?"

Panicking was out of the question and far past the point of helping, not that it ever did. She'd been tracked and found too many times by the vultures to get worked up now. No, now was time for clear thinking and a plan.

Help the injured.

Lark slid off the table quickly and grabbed for her shirt. She pulled it on and then ran behind the bar to grab clean towels and a bottle of vodka. She hurried toward a man she knew by name to be one of Keonae's triplet brothers. She put her hand over Aeson's on his stomach, and he collapsed forward, nearly knocking her to the ground in the process.

She went to her knees and applied pressure to his wound, handing the bottle of alcohol to Rossi. "This will help him. Give him a drink."

Rossi stared down at his brother in horror. "They butchered him and have packed his wounds with human soil."

She shook her head, not following.

Lazar's expression hardened. "Human soil stops our healing and infects our wounds. It must be cleansed at once or the damage will not heal. Much like what happened to Keonae long ago."

She held her breath a moment and looked up to find Keonae storming toward the bar's front door. He thrust Sachin aside and grabbed the handle. Everything in his stance said he was going off half-cocked and that while he may do some damage, he'd probably get himself killed.

She cried out, drawing his attention to her. "Jackass, calm down a minute here. Obviously, there are more of them than you guys or they wouldn't have run back in here. I've bumped into enough bird guys in my life to know none of you are wimps."

Sachin tipped his head, pondering her words. "She is correct. Their numbers are great. And we are weaponless, save this one I took from one I just killed. I believe Lazar killed another before grabbing Aeson. So there are now two less of them to worry upon, but still more than us."

Rossi bent and began pouring the

alcohol over Aeson's wounds, making the man on the floor scream in agony. Rossi kept going, but looked pained by the action. "We would have had weapons if you'd have let us leave the realm with them."

Lazar touched Rossi's shoulder. "What is done is done. Let us focus on a way out of this."

Lark bent her head a moment and then squared her shoulders, her gaze locking on Rossi. They needed help in the form of weapons and she could offer it. "Can you see to Aeson?"

He nodded.

"Use all the liquor you need, okay?"

He nodded again. "What of you?"

She stood, blood coating her hands. She wiped them on her shirt, unconcerned with how she now looked. She'd seen blood before. A lot of it. Sometimes it felt as if her life was drenched in it. She went right for Keonae and grabbed his hand, tugging on him, wanting him to follow. He did. She led him down the hall in the direction of the back door. She veered into the break room, where an old set of metal lockers lined one wall.

Without hesitation she pointed to the lockers. "Move them."

Keonae arched a brow in question, lost as to her request.

"Keon, move the lockers," she ordered. They didn't have time to spare. "I can, but I'm not as strong as you."

He did as she asked and she waited as he pushed the lockers out, exposing a whole in the wall behind them. She darted past him and squeezed into the opening, grabbing a large duffle bag she'd hid there the day after she'd started working. She dragged it out and slid it across the floor to his feet.

Keonae bent and when he opened the bag he gasped. "Lark, why do you have these?"

As he withdrew one of the many sheathed swords, she swallowed hard and reached in, grabbing a short sword. "I noticed guns weren't the most effective weapons of choice against them a long time ago."

"So you amassed a weapons collection?" he asked, shock in his voice.

"Sort of. This is a small sample of it. My apartment has a stash, a few locations around town have some. I have some in other cities and towns."

He stared at her, his expression blank.

She bit her inner lip. "This makes me look crazy, doesn't it?"

"Makes you prepared," he said, grabbed her, and kissed her before stepping back. "Now, find a place to hide while we handle the vultures."

She jerked. He was going to make her run and hide? She had a weapons stash that might save their asses and he wanted her to be a damsel in distress? She held her short sword tighter and rushed out behind him, ignoring his request. She wasn't about to let the vultures win.

Keonae and Sachin opened the main door and were out before she could reach them. She was just about to exit as well when Lazar spun and caught her.

"Stay. At best they will kill you," he said, his voice deep.

She struggled against his hold. "Listen, I get you guys have some backwards views on women, but I've been fighting and running from these things for most of my life. I'm not going to let them hurt the people I love."

"And these people you love would be?" he asked.

Her nostrils flared. "Keon. Fine. I love Keon. Now move it, bird boy."

He laughed, but didn't get out of her way. Instead, he grabbed her, lifted her, and then tossed her backwards into the air. Her stomach dropped and she nearly screamed, but strong arms caught her and eased her to her feet. She twisted in Rossi's arms.

"What the hell?"

He pointed to his brother on the floor. "He is trying to heal. Have you buckets for water? That may help."

She wanted to run out and fight, but one look at Aeson said he needed her more at the moment. "The employee bathroom has a crappy stand-up shower in it. It's old and right now it's packed with boxes of paperwork because it's an extra space, and I don't think the owner is much on housekeeping. I'm pretty sure the water works. We could clean him there."

Rossi bent and lifted his brother, looking strained, which said a lot about how much bird guys must weigh. She glanced to the doorway. Lazar was nowhere to be seen.

"Come. They will do what needs to be done," said Rossi. "We shall assist Aeson. He has a mate and young ones. His loss would be felt greatly."

"Sure, guilt me into helping," she mumbled, following behind him like a trained puppy.

———

KEONAE SPUN, weapon in hand, countering the oncoming blow. He barely registered the reverberation, his mind on a singular mission—protect Lark. He twisted, scoring a direct hit, the steel of his sword pressing through the flesh of his enemy with ease that was a testament to the sharp blade and his continued training.

As that enemy fell, he charged another and another, cutting through them as quickly. He wouldn't risk giving them time to get to Lark. The battle continued and Keonae realized the sheer number of the enemy far exceeded that which he'd seen in previous skirmishes. He glanced in Sachin's direction to find him engaged in a sword fight as well. Lazar no longer held a sword and was fighting hand-to-hand style with his opponents.

A vulture moved behind Lazar and Keonae bent, grabbing a discarded weapon and throwing it end over end at the vulture about to attack Lazar from behind. The sword burrowed deep into the enemy's chest and the man fell away as Lazar caught sight of him. Lazar nodded his thanks and kept fighting.

While it was three against many, they didn't stop or falter. Each knew the stakes. Kill or be killed. And none wanted to fall at the hands of the vultures. Keonae glanced to his side and caught sight of a group of vultures making their way into the bar. He tried to go for them but found himself locked in a sword fight against three opponents.

Sachin and Lazar were occupied as well. Keonae's gut tightened. Rossi would be left to defend Lark. If his baby brother failed, Keonae's mate would be in danger, possibly even killed.

Unacceptable!

He roared, attacking with blind rage and fury. What felt like an eternity passed before he had dispatched of the enemy outside and was able to run to the bar. He crashed through the back door, hitting the wall with more momentum than he'd planned. Ignoring the pain, he pushed onward, his intent to get to Lark.

"Oh shit!"

Keonae's gut tightened at the sound of Rossi's voice. He ran into the open area of the bar and stopped in his tracks when he found Lark standing there, holding two short swords, one in each hand, her long hair over one shoulder, her posture perfect as she stood over fallen vultures.

Blood pooled around the enemy and inched its way toward Lark's feet. She didn't budge. She glanced over her shoulder. "You're okay!"

He looked to Rossi, his mind struggling to process what he was seeing. Had his brother not been, who had killed the enemy?

Rossi pointed to Lark. "Your woman kicked their asses."

Keonae moved to her at a run and jerked her away from the puddle of blood. He put himself between her and the enemy even though rational thought dictated they were dead and would not rise and attack her. It didn't matter. He wanted her safe.

He removed the swords from her hands and gave her a stern look. "You were to allow my brother to protect you."

She huffed. "Well, next time I'm about to be attacked I'll be sure to wait for him to assist."

Keonae nodded, pleased she understood his orders. "Good."

"You're serious?"

Keonae glanced around. "Is this a time one would normally joke?"

"I'm totally into a complete Neanderthal."

Lazar and Sachin appeared, holding Aeson up between them. Aeson's color was returning somewhat. That was a good sign. It meant his wounds were healing.

"We should go," said Sachin. "There may be more coming."

"Go where?" asked Lark.

Keonae drew her closer. "You are coming home with me."

"Wait, you're returning to the kingdom?" asked Rossi.

Keonae replied. "Yes, and I am bringing my woman."

"What if I don't want to go?"

He stared hard at her.

She buckled. "Fine. I want to go. Don't look so menacing."

Chapter Nine

LARK STARED AROUND THE DIMLY LIT chamber. It was like something from a fantasy novel. It felt as if she'd traveled back in time and that any minute someone would lead her to the famed round table. In awe, she touched one of the thick wood tables near the door. On one sat a tray of fresh fruits and a decanter of wine. Several of the fruits were unlike any she'd ever seen before and she wondered if they were native to the realm. Two goblets were near. They looked like something from medieval times beautifully engraved with rare jewels around the sides. Her inner child wanted to use them and pretend to be royalty.

Gulping, she remembered the man

with her actually was royalty. Her quiet biker boy was really an ass-kicking, bird-shifting prince who just happened to be selected by gods she'd never heard of to be hers and hers alone. It was a lot to soak in.

She glanced over her shoulder. "I thought you said this was your room."

Keonae raked his gaze over her slowly. "It is."

"But it doesn't look like it's been used in years. It looks fresh, like it's never been left to dust or sit."

Keonae trailed a finger down the back of her arm lightly, causing a shiver to race through her. "It has not been used, but the castle staff sees to its upkeep."

"And the food and wine?" she questioned, leaning back against him, trying to focus on all the questions bubbling in her brain. The realm was new to her. Being in a castle wasn't something she'd experienced before, either. Especially not a functional, picture-perfect one. She wanted to savor it all, soak it all in. Sadly, it had been too dark to see anything on the flight here.

Flight.

She nearly laughed.

Flying had always been something done on a plane to her. But not now. Now she knew what it was like to be held by a powerful man as he soared high in the skies, his grip on her tight, yet not painful. She'd worried she be too much weight for him to fly with. That worry was silly now, especially considering the ease with which Keonae had done so.

She sank back against him, knowing the feel of his front pressed to her back by heart now—as it had been the way they'd flown here. He rubbed her arms fully.

"You are still cold," he said matter-of-factly.

It had been extremely cold on their journey. The men didn't seem to notice the bite of it, but she had. Thankfully, Keonae seemed to be a portable heater, radiating heat the entire flight.

She shivered again. "A little."

He breathed against her ear, his body tight against the back of hers. "But you are shaking."

Closing her eyes briefly, she lifted an

arm over her head, touching his scruffy cheek. "I think I'm nervous."

"You fear me?" He ran his fingertips down her inner exposed arm.

"No. Not at all." She turned in his arms and met his gaze. "Keon, you saved my life and you brought me here, to your realm."

He blinked. "It is your realm too. You are of a shifter line."

She wasn't explaining it very well and she knew as much. She tried again. "Keonae, you made it very clear what I am to you."

He touched her hip. "You are my mate."

"Right, and you saved me and brought me here—to your bedroom in *another realm*," she stressed, wondering if he'd get the hint.

"If my chambers within the castle are not to your liking, we can journey to my secondary home here. I have not been there in a very long time, but have been told it too is kept up in the event I have use of it," he said, his attention on her chest, not their conversation.

She laughed softly. "I'm trying to say that I'm nervous about what I know is about to happen. The claiming Lazar joked about on the way here."

Keonae's brows met. "You are afraid of being claimed fully by me?"

"I don't exactly understand what it entails, so a little, yes," she admitted.

The sides of his lips curved upward. "Pleasure, *ta'konima*. Nothing but pleasure. I assure you."

She let out a breath she'd been unaware she'd been holding. Well, at least that part was out of the way. Though her nerves didn't settle. She'd been with men before. Lark wouldn't venture so far as to label herself experienced, but she wasn't a blushing virgin. Still, Keonae wasn't like other men. There was a primal rawness to him that warned her that joining with him would be unlike anything she'd done before.

He cupped her face, his lips brushing over hers. "I have sent word for my bathing chambers to be readied for you and me, if you want for me to join you."

"You have your own bathing chambers?" she questioned, unsure why she was surprised. The guy was a frigging prince after all.

"I do."

She paused. "We should check on Aeson again. Those doctor guys seemed a little sketchy."

He grinned. "They are healers and they are well-trained in how to assist him. He is in good hands."

"Are you sure? The one guy lit a bundle of herbs and started to chant. I don't think that is exactly cutting-edge medicine."

His response was a kiss. A toe-curling, back-bending one that made her moan into his mouth. She ran her hands over his bare chest, happy he'd not covered it when they'd landed. He slowed their kiss as his muscles tightened under the weight of her touch. She knew why. He wanted to hide himself from her.

She pushed on him hard, her intention

to knock a little sense into him. He stumbled backwards and hit the huge wooden door. His eyes widened and then stark possessiveness shone from their depths. It was on the tip of her tongue to scold him for wanting to shy away from her, but her body picked then to respond to his silent plea for more.

She went at him, her mouth finding his, her hands roaming over his muscles and his scars. Damn, but the man would soon realize she thought he was perfect if she had to hit him over the head with one of those swords he was so fond of.

Keonae tugged at her shirt, and she broke the kiss long enough to remove it. He grabbed her bra and tore it from her body as if it were no more than tissue paper between them. Her already cold nipples were erect and his gaze fixed upon them. She shook her head, kissing her way down his neck then his torso until she reached the top of his jeans.

He tried to step forward and pull her upward. Lark shook her head and used her strength to keep him pinned to the door, strongly suspecting he was allowing her the small victory. She'd seen him in action. He was strong enough to move her.

She opened his jeans and smiled at the sight of his cock barely contained within them. It had dug at her back and butt the entire flight to the castle, so she already knew it would be big. Seeing it up close and personal was something altogether different.

"Oh wow," she whispered, kissing a line to the patch of well-kept hair at his cock base.

Keonae stiffened and hit the door with one hand, his palm splayed there on the wood. She feared he'd break the thing down and they'd end up on their asses in the open hallway for all to see.

"Lark," he said, his voice low, his cock bobbing before her lips. She lowered his jeans more, freeing him fully.

She took the tip of him into her mouth and stared up at his face through hooded lashes. His long, thick and hard cock was more than she could fully take with her mouth, so she added her hands, wrapping her fingers around his shaft, making him stiffen more.

He shouted something in his native language, and from the looks of it, whatever he said meant he was enjoying himself. Pride welled and she took him as deep as she could in her mouth, her hands easing up and down the length of him, her saliva slicking his velvety-smooth erection. His hips began to thrust gently and she let him lead, fucking her mouth, her body on fire with need for him. She wanted to please him, make him come harder than he ever had before. She wanted him to know that to her he was the single, sexiest man she'd ever met and ever would meet.

Keonae thumped the back his head against the door and shouted again, still saying things she didn't understand but sensed were good. There was banging from the other side of the door and she paused her actions, keeping his cock in her mouth.

"My lord?" asked a man from the hall. "Is all well, sir?"

"Go…away," ground out Keonae

through clenched teeth, his hands finding the sides of her head before lacing through her hair. He pulled at her, pushing deeper into her mouth. "By the gods, woman. You are magik."

She raked her teeth over his shaft lightly, drawing a fierce growl from him. One moment she was bent before him, and the next he had her lifted in the air. He set her down for just a second, tearing off his boots and jeans, and then grabbing her. Lifting her, he stalked in the direction of the ornate bed. He plopped her onto the bed and she bounced up once and laughed.

Keonae's expression held no humor. Only lust. The man was about to take what was his and she couldn't have been happier. He made short work of her shoes and jeans and then took forever drawing her panties down the length of her legs.

"Keon," she yelled, wanting him to move faster, to take her and claim her already.

He bent his head, kissing the top of her mound. A thin strip of hair was all she kept there, and he kissed his way around it, exploring her, driving her mad with need.

She bucked, wanting him to take her fully. The aggravating man slowed and had the nerve to chuckle against her inner thigh. With a huff, she propped herself on her elbows, glaring down at his head between her legs.

He spread her thighs wide and buried his face there, sending her mind into a dither. She forgot about being angry with him for taking his time and teasing her. All that filled her head was bliss. Lark wasn't sure how long he remained there. It felt as if hours had passed with him taking her so close to the edge of culmination and then easing back, taunting her, keeping her pleasure just out of reach.

"K-Keonae," she managed, her entire body spent as if she'd run a marathon rather than lying there writhing with passion.

His lips glistened as he looked up at her. "Lark, do you accept me? All of me from now until the end of time?"

What the hell kind of question was

that? She wanted him buried deep in her and he was stopping to ask her something like that. With a grunt of frustration, she responded. "Of course I do, biker boy. Now fuck me."

"Not until you say you accept me."

She snarled.

He grinned.

Damn him.

"I accept you," she ground out.

He bent his head and tweaked her swollen bud just right, sending her body crashing into her zenith. She shook, everything on her buzzing with pleasure as he rose up and positioned himself between her legs. Keonae met her gaze and then impaled her sweetly, driving himself balls deep, making her cry out as more pleasure racked her body. Numbness started in her toes and worked its way up, her body moving from numb to prickling pleasure to numb again.

The man was trying to kill her with sex and he was close to succeeding. There was a buzzing and then it felt as if pure energy rushed from him to her and back again.

Gasping, she clung to his arms, arching her back, the walls of her pussy clutching his cock. He jerked against her, and there was no mistaking his orgasm. He tossed his head back, shouting as he released in her, their bodies finding pleasure in one another yet again.

Keonae shook slightly as he leaned down, his body fully on hers, yet not crushing her. He kissed her lips tenderly. "You are mine now, Lark. My mate. My wife."

She had done nothing but worry on their journey here, wondering what the claiming would entail, worried she'd let him down somehow. Now she couldn't imagine not being tied to him. She touched the scars on his cheek and then kissed him there.

"Does this mean it's unbreakable?" she asked. "The bond with us?"

"Yes," he said kissing the tips of her fingers. "You are mine forever."

Sadness swept over her, stealing her joy. "But they'll keep coming for me."

He pushed into her more, his cock

renewed with life even though they'd just finished. "They will not get to you. I stand in their path, as does my kingdom."

"I don't want you hurt on my account," she said, pushing on his chest, wanting to talk with him and get this out of the way. "Aeson was already hurt because they came looking for me."

"He was hurt because they are evil. Not because of you," he said, pushing in all the way and swiveling his hips just so, making her gasp as pleasure shot through her lower region. "We shall speak of it no more. Be ice."

She tipped her head. "Huh?"

"Um, be cool?"

She didn't want to laugh at him, but she couldn't help it. "Ah. Okay, yes. Be cool. Not be ice."

"Noted."

"Keon."

"Yes?"

She wrapped her legs around his waist tightly. "I love you."

"Good, because I love you and plan to beget you with my babes," he said, rolling onto his back, taking her with him, planting her on top of him. "Now, woman, ride me."

She laughed as she bent, moving on his cock as he instructed. "Bossy biker boy."

"Take every inch of my cock, woman. I plan to join with you until the morning light comes. And then, perhaps, until nightfall again." He slapped her ass cheek playfully. "Ride me faster. I wish to savor the sight of you above me."

"Yes, sir," she said with a wink, taking him deeper.

Chapter Ten

KEONAE STARED LOVINGLY AT HIS MATE AS she toweled off from their morning bath. The expressions she'd made upon seeing his private bathing chamber would stay with him for a long time. He liked spoiling her. She worked too hard, and from the little bit she'd confessed to him, she'd spent most of her time running from vultures. She deserved the life he could offer her. He still wasn't sure what his reception would be from the people of the Hawks' kingdom. They could very well want him gone once more. Kabril seemed to think they would welcome him with open arms.

Keonae wasn't so sure. All that he wanted to worry upon for the moment was his new bride. She looked even more beautiful to him in the first light of day. He had taken her more times than he could count, and still his cock wanted to return to her silken depths. "You're stunning."

A blush stole across her cheeks. "Stop."

"But you are."

She blinked up at him, holding the towel around her. He no longer felt the need to cover himself from her view and stood there, fully naked, his hand on his cock as he stroked it, watching her. Her gaze snapped to his erection. "I think he's had enough for a bit."

"Never."

She beamed. "Okay, but I need a small break."

"Very well," he said with a mock sigh, pulling her closer to him with his free hand. He kissed her passionately, leaving no room for doubt on his feelings for her.

When he stopped, she put her cheek to his chest. "Keon, we need to check on Aeson."

"He is doing well," replied Keonae.

"The serving wench who brought the food to break our fast mentioned as much."

Lark gave him a stern look. "Serving wench?"

He waited, unsure what had set her off.

She sighed. "Never mind. We'll deal with your choice of terms later. I heard her talking to you but didn't understand what she was saying. She had news about Aeson?"

He nodded, still stroking himself lazily. "The healers have allowed Aeson's mate to be near him. Shelby reassured everyone that Aeson is doing much better. She says he is barking orders at the healers. A very good sign."

She smiled wide. "Good!"

He put an arm around her and nuzzled his face to her neck, inhaling her scent. "I want to be in you again."

She took over stroking his cock. "I know, but I'm sore and you're going to have to wait. In the meantime, I'm dying to see the realm. Can we go outside, please?"

He chuckled. "Of course. Come. Look

upon the kingdom as the light shines at the start of the day."

She tugged on him. "We're not dressed. I don't have any clothes. You ripped mine."

"Clothing is being gathered for you as we speak. And no clothes are necessary. It is far too early for anyone to be out and about, and we are high up. Plus, this side of the castle faces mostly wooded area. None will see you."

She looked hesitant but nodded. "Okay, but I'm keeping the towel. I don't want some random guy flying past and seeing my lady bits."

He laughed. "I would like to see your lady bits."

"You've seen all my lady bits," she returned suggestively.

He waggled his brows. "I know and I want to see them again."

"Keon, you're terrible," she said with a laugh, kissing his shoulder and releasing his cock.

He groaned and tugged lightly at the top of the towel. "A great terrible beast?"

"You wish." She held tight to the towel and pointed to the double doors she suspected led to the balcony he'd spoken of. "If you don't show me this realm, I'm going to rip off your man bits."

He took her hand and snorted as he covered the distance to the doors. He tossed them open and faced her, walking backwards onto the large half circle balcony. He put his arms out wide, his wings emerging from his back as he did. He stood before her naked, his wings out fully, grinning.

"You look like the cat that ate the canary," she said, laughing at his playful side. It was good to see him smile and laugh.

He tipped his head. "Why would I eat a canary? I know hawks from the human realm eat smaller birds and prey, but to us here, eating a bird is a form of cannibalism. We avoid it, and canaries are so petite in comparison to us. That kingdom is full of very small people."

She covered her mouth and did her

best to avoid laughing. "My mistake. You look like you're up to no good."

He backed up more, flapping his wings as he did. He opened his mouth but whatever he was about to say was completely drowned out by the roar of what sounded like hundreds of people.

Lark froze.

So did Keonae.

There was a scuffle behind them and Lark turned to find Rossi there, his gaze averted from her as he felt his way out onto the balcony. "For the love of the bird gods, why would you greet the people of our kingdom naked?"

Keonae remained in place, his wings out, his back to what Lark was fast suspecting was more than hundreds. His gaze hardened on his brother. "Greet the people?"

Rossi stilled. "Wait, I sent Lazar to tell you Kabril announced you were home and that our subjects were gathered in celebration, waiting for you to step out and greet them. And Kabril may have let it slip you found your mate."

Lark gasped. "Lazar never showed."

Rossi glanced at her, his face ashen, and then he looked away fast. "Shit."

The crowd cheered louder and some began to whistle. Lark lost it, unable to hide her laughter. Keonae's face was unreadable, and she realized he was worried about how they would view him—that they'd not seen him since he'd gotten the scars.

More whistled.

She kept hold of her towel and stayed back, hoping to be out of view of the people below. "Biker boy, sounds to me like they think you're as sexy as I do."

Keonae's cheeks reddened and he squared his shoulders. She thought he'd dart in past her. When he boldly turned to face the people of his kingdom, still naked, his wings out, his hands cupping his groin as best he could, she clapped, so proud of him for overcoming his inner demons that she forgot she was in just a towel.

It slipped away, pooling at her feet. The crowd whistled more and cheered louder. Gasping, she reached for the towel as Keonae glanced over his shoulder. Shocked, he reached for her, uncovering himself.

Rossi tossed his hands in the air. "Oh, come on, you two!"

Lark and Keonae bumped heads. She touched her forehead as he yanked the towel up and covered her front from view.

Someone cleared their throats behind her and she wanted to crawl in and under the large bed. "I came in hopes of being introduced to your mate."

The voice sounded just like Keonae's.

She didn't dare turn around.

Rossi smiled wide. "Lark, I would like to introduce you to our eldest brother—the king. Kabril, this is Lark. You already know the fool with her."

"Shit," said Lark, stealing Rossi's favorite curse word.

Keonae groaned. "Could everyone give us a moment, please?"

"We would, but it seems rather point-less as you have gifted the entire kingdom a view of you in nothing more than what you were born in," said Kabril.

Lark wiggled to get the towel around her and turned, darting into the room, past the man who looked just like Aeson and Keonae. She dove under the covers on the bed, making the king laugh.

Cringing, she peeked out to find Keonae standing there unabashed, his wings folding into him and then vanishing altogether. He crossed his arms over his chest. "Brother, would you like me to see your mate's bare bottom?"

The smile faded from Kabril's face. He snapped his fingers at Rossi. "Shut the doors and leave them be for now. We shall try this again in an hour, when they have hopefully found the clothing we sent with Lazar."

"I am going to kill him," said Keonae.

Rossi smirked. "I have to hand it to him, this was his best prank yet."

Lark covered her head, embarrassed beyond belief.

"We have mated, so I suspect the queen will wish to have a celebration," said Keonae.

"Oh, Brother, congratulations," said

Kabril. "Rayna will be beside herself. I will find Lazar and the clothing he was to bring you. And, Lark, welcome to the family."

Rossi laughed. "We should lie and tell her every day is like this."

"It is as though you want me to kill you," said Keonae, a light tone to his voice. "Be gone before I decide to do so."

"I'm going, I'm going," chimed Rossi.

The door shut.

Lark remained under the covers. "I can't show my face here again."

"I would prefer you not show your lady bits again. Your face is more than welcome to be shown," said Keonae laughing.

THE END

About the Author

Dear Reader

Did you enjoy this title and want to know more about Mandy M. Roth, her pen names and all the titles she has available for purchase (over 100)?

About Mandy:

New York Times & *USA TODAY* Bestselling Author Mandy M. Roth is a self-proclaimed Goonie, loves 80s music and movies and wishes leg warmers would come back into fashion. She also thinks the movie The Breakfast Club should be mandatory viewing for...okay, everyone. When she's not dancing around her office to the sounds of the 80s or writing books, she can be found designing book covers for New York publishers, small presses, and indie authors.

Learn More:

To learn more about Mandy and her pen names, please visit www.MandyRoth.com

For latest news about Mandy's newest releases and sales subscribe to her newsletter: Sign Up For Mandy's Newsletter

Want to see all Mandy's books? Click here.

Printable PDF list of all Mandy's titles: Click here.

To join Mandy's Facebook Reader Group: The Roth Heads.

Review this title:

Please let others know if you enjoyed this title. Consider leaving an honest review on the vendor site in which you purchased this title. Reviews help to spread the word and boost overall sales. This means more books in the series you love.

Thank you!

facebook.com/AuthorMandyRoth

twitter.com/mandymroth

instagram.com/mandymroth

goodreads.com/mandymroth

pinterest.com/mandymroth

bookbub.com/authors/mandy-m-roth

youtube.com/mandyroth

amazon.com/author/mandyroth

Featured Titles from Mandy
M. Roth

The Immortal Ops Series World
Immortal Ops
Critical Intelligence
Radar Deception
Strategic Vulnerability
Tactical Magik
Act of Mercy
Administrative Control
Act of Surrender
Broken Communication
Separation Zone
Act of Submission
Damage Report
Act of Command
Wolf's Surrender
The Dragon Shifter's Duty

Midnight Echoes

Isolated Maneuver

Expecting Darkness

Area of Influence

Act of Passion

Act of Brotherhood

Healing the Wolf

Wrecked Intel

And more to come…

Cozy Paranormal Mysteries

Once Hunted, Twice Shy

Total Eclipse of the Hunt

Don't Stop Bewitching

And more to come…

Tempting Fate Series

Loup Garou

Bad Moon Rising

And more to come…

The Guardians Series

The Guardians

Crossing Hudson

Ruling Jude

And more to come…

The Druid Series

Sacred Places

Goddess of the Grove

Winter Solstice

A Druid of Her Own

And more to come…

The King of Prey Series

King of Prey

A View to a Kill

Master of the Hunt

Rise of the King

Prince of Pleasure

Prince of Flight

Bureau of Paranormal Investigation (BPI)

Hunted Holiday

Heated Holiday

Prospect Springs Shifters

Blaze of Glory

Parker's Honor

Gabe's Fortune

CPSIA information can be obtained
at www.ICGtesting.com
Printed in the USA
LVOW10s1550230518
578229LV00001B/206/P